# WHAT THE GREEK'S MONEY CAN'T BUY

BY

MAYA BLAKE

First published in Great Britain 2014
by Mills & Boon, an imprint of Harlequin (UK) Limited,
Large Print edition 2014
Eton House, 18-24 Paradise Road,
Richmond, Surrey, TW9 1SR



ISBN: 978-0-263-24086-3

Harlequin (UK) Limited's policy is to use papers that are natural, renewable and recyclable products and made from wood grown in sustainable forests. The logging and manufacturing processes conform to the legal environmental regulations of the country of origin.

Printed and bound in Great Britain
by CPI Antony Rowe, Chippenham, Wiltshire

# WHAT THE GREEK'S MONEY CAN'T BUY

# CHAPTER ONE

'COME ON, PUT your back into it! Why am I not surprised that you're slacking as usual while I'm doing all the work?'

Sakis Pantelides reefed the oars through the slightly choppy water, loving the exhilaration and adrenaline that burned in his back and shoulders. 'Stop complaining, old man. It's not my fault if you're feeling your age.' He smiled when he heard his brother's hiss of annoyance.

In truth, Ari was only two-and-a-half years older, but Sakis knew it annoyed him when he taunted him with their age difference, so of course he never passed up the chance to niggle where he could.

'Don't worry, Theo will be around to bail you out next time we row. That way you won't have to *strain* yourself so much,' Sakis said.

'Theo would be more concerned about showing off his bulging muscles to the female coxes than he would to serious rowing,' Ari responded dryly. 'How he ever managed to stop showing off long enough to win five world championships, I'll never know.'

Sakis heaved his oars and noted with satisfaction that he hadn't lost the innate rhythm despite several months away from the favourite sport that had at one time been his sole passion. Thinking about his younger brother, he couldn't help but smile. 'Yeah, he always *was* more into his looks and the ladies than anything else.'

He rowed in perfect sync with his brother, their movements barely rippling through the water as they passed the halfway point of the lake used by the exclusive rowing club a few miles outside of London. Sakis's smile widened as a sense of peace stole over him.

It'd been a while since he'd come here; since he'd found time to connect with his brothers like this. The punishing schedules it took to manage the three branches of Pantelides Inc meant the brothers hadn't got together in way too long. That they had even been in the same time zone had been a miracle. Of course, it hadn't stayed that way for long. Theo had cancelled at the last minute and was right this moment winging his way to Rio on a Pantelides jet to deal with a crisis for the global conglomerate.

Or maybe Theo had cancelled for another reason altogether.

His playboy brother wasn't above flying thousands of miles for a one-hour dinner date with a beautiful woman. 'If I find out he blew us off for a piece of skirt, I'll confiscate his plane for a month.'

Ari snorted. 'You can try. But I think you're asking for a swift death if you attempt to come between Theo and a woman. Speaking of women, I see yours has finally managed to surgically remove herself from her laptop…'

He didn't break his rhythm despite the jolt of electricity that zapped through him. His gaze focused past his brother's shoulder to where Ari's attention was fixed.

He nearly missed his next stroke. Only the inbuilt discipline that had seen him win one more championship than his brothers' five apiece stopped him from losing his rhythm.

'Let's get one thing straight—she's *not* my woman.'

Brianna Moneypenny, his executive assistant, stood next to his car. That in itself was a surprise, since she preferred to stay glued to his in-limo computer, one finger firmly on the pulse of his company any time he had to step away.

But what triggered the bolt of astonishment in

him more was the not-quite-masked expression on her face. Brianna's countenance since the day she'd become his ultra-efficient assistant eighteen months ago had never once wavered from cool, icy professionalism.

Today she looked…

'Don't tell me she's succumbed to the Sakis Pantelides syndrome?' Ari's dry tone held equal parts amusement and resignation.

Sakis frowned, unease stirring in his belly and mingling with the emotions he refused to acknowledge when it came to his executive assistant. He'd learned the hard way that exposing emotion, especially for the wrong person, could leave scars that never really healed and took monumental effort to keep buried. As for mixing business with pleasure—that had been a near lethal cocktail he'd sampled once. Never again. 'Shut up, Ari.'

'I'm concerned, brother. She's almost ready to jump into the water. Or jump your bones, more like. Please tell me you haven't lost your mind and slept with her?'

Sakis's gaze flitted over to Moneypenny, trying to pinpoint what was wrong from across the distance between them. 'I'm not sure what's more disturbing—your unhealthy interest in my sex life or the fact that you can keep rowing straight while practising the Spanish Inquisition,' he murmured absently.

As for getting physical with Moneypenny, if his libido chose the most inappropriate times—like now—to remind him he was a red-blooded male, it was a situation he intended to keep ignoring, like he had been the last eighteen months. He'd wasted too much valuable time in this lifetime ridding himself of clinging women.

He strained the oars through the water, suddenly wanting the session to be over. Through the strokes, he kept his gaze fixed on Moneypenny, her rigid stance setting off alarm bells inside his head.

'So, there's nothing between you two?' Ari pushed.

Something in his brother's voice made his hackles rise. With one last push, he felt the bottom of the scull hit the slope of the wooden jetty.

'If you're thinking of trying to poach her, Ari, forget it. She's the best executive assistant I've ever had and anyone who threatens that will lose a body part; two body parts for family members.'

'Cool your jets, bro. I wasn't thinking of that sort of poaching. Besides, hearing you gush over her like that tells me you're already far gone.'

Sakis's irritation grew, wishing his brother would get off the subject.

'Just because I recognise talent doesn't mean I've lost my mind. Besides, tell me, does *your* assistant know her Windsor knot from her double-cross knot?'

Ari's brows shot up as he stepped onto the pier and grabbed his oars. 'My assistant is a man. And the fact that you hired yours based on her tie-knotting abilities only confirms you're more screwed than I thought.'

'There's nothing delusional about the fact that she has more brains in her pinkie than the total sum of my previous assistants, and she's a Rottweiler when it comes to managing my business life. That's all I need.'

'Are you sure that's all? Because I detect a distinct…*reverence* in your tone there.'

Sakis froze, then grimaced when he realised Ari was messing with him. 'Keep it up. I owe you a scar for the one you planted on me with your carelessness.' He touched the arrow-shaped scar just above his right brow, a present from Ari's oar when they had first started rowing together in their teens.

'Someone had to bring you down a notch or three for thinking you were the better-looking brother.' Ari grinned, and Sakis was reminded of the carefree brother Ari had been before tragedy had struck and sunk its merciless claws into him. Then Ari's gaze slid beyond Sakis's shoulder. 'Your Rottweiler's prowling for you. She looks ready to bare her teeth.'

Sakis dropped his oars next to the overturned scull and glanced over, to find Brianna had moved closer. She now stood at the top of the pier, her arms folded and her gaze trained on him.

His alarm intensified. There was a look on her face he'd never seen before. Plus she held a towel in one hand, which suggested she was expecting him not to take his usual shower at the clubhouse.

Sakis frowned. 'Something's up. I need to go.'

'Did she communicate that to you subliminally or are you two so attuned to each other you can tell just by looking at her?' Ari enquired in an amused tone.

'Seriously, Ari, cork it.' His scowl deepened as he noted Brianna's pinched look. Again acting out of the ordinary, she started towards him.

Moneypenny knew never to disturb him during his time with his brothers. She was great like that. She knew her place in his life and had never once overstepped the mark. He started to walk away from the waterfront.

'Hey, don't worry about me. I'll make sure the equipment is returned to the boathouse. And I'll have all those drinks we ordered by myself too,' Ari stated drolly.

Sakis ignored him. When he reached speaking distance, he stopped. 'What's wrong?' he demanded.

For the very first time since she'd turned up for an interview at Pantelides Towers at five o'clock in the morning, Sakis saw her hesitate. The hair on his nape rose to attention. 'Spit it out, Moneypenny.'

The tightening of her mouth was infinitesimal but he spotted it. Another first. He couldn't remember ever witnessing an outward sign of distress. Silently, she held out his towel.

He snatched it from her, more to hurry her response than a need to wipe his sweat-drenched body.

'Mr Pantelides, we have a situation.'

His jaw tightened. 'What situation?'

'One of your tankers, the Pantelides Six, has run aground off Point Noire.'

Ice cascaded down his back despite the midsummer sun blazing down on him. Sakis forced a swallow. 'When did this happen?'

'I got a call via the head office from a crew member five minutes ago.'

She licked her lips and his apprehension grew.

‘There’s something else?’

‘Yes. The captain and two crew members are missing and…’

‘And what?’

Her pinched look intensified. ‘The tanker hit an outcropping of rocks. Crude oil is spilling into the South Atlantic at an estimated rate of sixty barrels per minute.’

Brianna would never forget what happened next after her announcement. Outwardly, Sakis Pantelides remained the calm, ruthlessly controlled oil tycoon she’d worked alongside for the past eighteen months. But she would’ve failed in her task to make herself indispensable to him if she hadn’t learned to read between the lines of the enigma that was Sakis Pantelides. The set of his strong jaw and the way his hands tightened around the snow-white towel told her how badly the news had affected him.

Over his shoulder, Brianna saw Arion Pantelides pause in his task. Her eyes connected with his. Something in her face must have given her away because before she’d taken another breath the oldest Pantelides brother was striding towards them. He was just as imposing as his younger brother, just as formidable. But, where Sakis’s gaze was sharp with laser-like focus and almost lethal intelligence, Arion's held a wealth of dark torment and soul-deep weariness.

Brianna's gaze swung back to her boss, and she wasn't even slightly surprised to see the solid mask of power and ruthless efficiency back in place.

'Do we know what caused the accident?' he fired out.

She shook her head. 'The captain isn't responding to his mobile phone. We haven't been able to establish contact with vessel since the initial call. The Congolese coast guard are on their way. I've asked them to contact me as soon as they're on site.' She fell into step beside him as his long strides headed for the car. 'I've got our emergency crew on standby. They're ready to fly out once you give the word.'

Arion Pantelides caught up with them as they neared the limousine.

He put a halting hand on his brother's shoulder. 'Talk to me, Sakis.'

In clipped tones, Sakis filled him in on what had happened. Arion's gaze swung to her. 'Do we have the names of the missing crew members?'

'I've emailed the complete crew manifest to both your phones and Theo's. I've also attached a list of the relevant ministers we need to deal with in the government to ensure we don't ruffle any feathers, and I've scheduled calls with all of them.'

A look flickered in his eyes before his gaze connected with his brother's. When Sakis's brow rose a fraction, Arion gave a small smile.

'Go. I'll deal with as much as I can from here. We'll talk in one hour.' Arion clasped his brother's shoulder in reassurance before he strode off.

Sakis turned to her. 'I'll need to speak to the President.'

Brianna nodded. 'I've got his chief of staff on hold. He'll put you through when you're ready.'

Her gaze dropped to his chest and immediately shifted away. She stepped back to move away from the potent scent of sweat and man that radiated off his deep olive skin. 'You need to change. I'll get you some fresh clothes.'

As she headed towards the boot of the car, she heard the slide of his rowing suit zip. She didn't turn because she'd seen it all before. At least that was what she told herself. She hadn't seen Sakis Pantelides totally naked, of course. But hers was a twenty-four-seven job. And, when you worked as close as she did with a suave, self-assured, powerful tycoon who saw you as nothing but a super-efficient, sexless automaton, you were bound to be exposed to all aspects of his nature. And his various states of undress.

The first time Sakis Pantelides had undressed in front of her, Brianna had taken it in her stride, just as she'd brutally trained herself to take most things in her stride.

To feel, to trust, to give emotion an inch, was to invite disaster.

So she'd learned to harden her heart. It had been that...or sink beneath the weight of crushing despair.

*And she refused to sink...*

She straightened from the boot with a pristine blue shirt and a charcoal-grey Armani suit in one hand and the perfectly knotted double Oxford tie Sakis favoured in the other. She kept her gaze trained on the sun-dappled lake beyond his shoulder as she handed the items over and went to retrieve his socks and hand-made leather shoes.

She didn't need to see his strong neck and shoulders, honed perfectly from his years of professional, championship-winning rowing, or his deep, ripped chest with silky hairs that arrowed down to his neat, trim waist and disappeared beneath the band of his boxers. She most certainly didn't need to see the powerful thighs that looked as if they could crush an unwary opponent, or pin a willing female to an unyielding wall…in the right circumstances. And she especially didn't need to see the black cotton boxer briefs that made a poor effort to contain his—

A loud beep signalling an incoming call from the limo's phone startled her into dropping his socks. She hastily picked them up and slid into the car. From the corner of her eye, she saw Sakis step into his trousers. Silently, she held out the remaining items and picked up the phone.

'Pantelides Shipping,' she said into the receiver as she picked up her electronic tablet. She listened calmly to the voice at the other end of the line, tapping away at her keyboard as she added to the ever-growing to-do list.

By the time Sakis slid next to her, and slammed the door, impeccably dressed, she was on her fifth item. She paused long enough to secure her seat belt before resuming her typing.

'The only answer I have for you right now is no comment. Sorry, no can do.' Sakis stiffened beside her. 'Absolutely not. No news outlet will be getting exclusives. Pantelides Shipping will issue one press release within the hour. It will be posted on our company's website and affiliated media and social network links with the relevant contact details. If you have any questions after that, contact our press office.'

'Tabloid or mainstream media?' Sakis asked the moment she hung up.

'Fleet Street. They want to verify what they've heard.' The phone rang again. Seeing the number of another tabloid, she ignored it. Sakis had more pressing phone calls to make. She passed him the headset connected to the call she'd put on hold for the last ten minutes.

The tightening of his jaw was almost imperceptible before complete control slid back into place. His fingers brushed hers as he took the device from her. The unnerving voltage that came from touching Sakis made her heartbeat momentarily fluctuate but that was yet another thing she took in her stride.

His deep voice brimmed with authority and bone-deep assuredness. It held the barest hint of his Greek heritage but Brianna knew he spoke his mother tongue with the same stunning fluency and efficiency with which he ran the crude-oil brokerage arm of Pantelides Shipping, his family's multibillion-dollar conglomerate.

'Mr President, please allow me to express my deepest regret at the situation we find ourselves in. Of course, my company takes full responsibility for this incident and will make every effort to ensure minimal ecological and economic distress. Yes, I have a fifty-man expert salvage and investigation crew on its way. They'll assess what needs to be done… Yes, I agree. I'll be there at the site within the next twelve hours.'

Brianna's fingers flew over her tablet as she absorbed the conversation and planned accordingly. By the time Sakis concluded the call, she had his private jet and necessary flight crew on standby.

They both stopped as the sleek phone rang again.

'Would you like me to get it?' Brianna asked.

Sakis shook his head. 'No. I'm the head of the company. The buck stops with me.' His gaze snagged hers with a compelling look that held hers captive. 'This is going to get worse before it gets better. Are you up to the task, Miss Moneypenny?'

Brianna forced herself to breathe, even as the tingle in her shoulder reminded her of the solemn vow she'd taken in a dark, cold room two years ago.

*I refuse to sink.*

She swallowed and firmed her spine. 'Yes, I'm up to the task, Mr Pantelides.'

Dark-green eyes the colour of fresh moss held hers for a moment longer. Then he gave a curt nod and picked up the phone.

'Pantelides,' he clipped out.

For the rest of the journey to Pantelides Towers, Brianna immersed herself in doing what she did best—anticipating her boss's every need and fulfilling it without so much as a whisper-light ruffle.

It was the only way she knew how to function nowadays.

By the time she handed their emergency suitcases to his helicopter pilot and followed Sakis into the lift that would take them to the helipad at the top of Pantelides Towers, they had a firm idea of what lay ahead of them.

There was nothing they could do to stop the crude oil spilling into the South Atlantic—at least not until the salvage team got there and went into action.

But, glancing at him, Brianna knew it wasn't only the disaster that had put the strain on Sakis's face. It was also being hit with the unexpected.

If there was one thing Sakis hated, it was surprises. It was why he always out-thought his opponents by a dozen moves, so he couldn't be surprised. Having gained a little insight into his past from working with him, Brianna wasn't surprised.

The devastating bombshell Sakis's father had dropped on his family when Sakis had been a teen was still fodder for journalists. Of course, she didn't know the full story, but she knew enough to understand why Sakis would hate having his company thrown into the limelight like this.

His phone rang again.

'Mrs Lowell. No, I'm sorry, there's no news.' His voice held the strength and the solid dependable calm needed to reassure the wife of the missing captain. 'Yes, he's still missing, but please be assured, I'll personally call you as soon as I have any information. You have my word.'

A pulse jumped in his temple as he hung up. 'How long before the search and rescue team are at the site?'

She checked her watch. 'Ninety minutes.'

'Hire another crew. Three teams working in eight-hour shifts are better than two working in twelve-hour shifts. I don't want anything missed because they're exhausted. And they're to work around the clock until the missing crew are found. Make it happen, Moneypenny.'

'Yes, of course.'

The lift doors opened. Brianna nearly stumbled when his hand settled in the small of her back to guide her out.

In all her time working for him, he'd never touched her in any way. Forcing herself not to react, she glanced at him. His face was set, his brows clamped in fierce concentration as he guided her swiftly towards the waiting helicopter. A few feet away, his hand dropped. He waited for the pilot to help her up into her seat before he slid in beside her.

Before the aircraft was airborne, Sakis was on the phone again, this time to Theo. The urgent exchange in Greek went right over Brianna's head but it didn't stop her secret fascination with the mellifluous language or the man who spoke it.

His glance slid to her and she realised she'd been unashamedly staring.

She snapped her attention back to the tablet in her hand and activated it.

There'd been nothing personal in Sakis's touch or his look. Not that she'd expected there to be. In all ways and in all things, Sakis Pantelides was extremely professional.

She expected nothing less from him. And that was just the way she wished it.

Her lesson had been well and truly learned in that department, in the harshest possible way, barring death—not that she hadn't come close once or twice. And all because she'd allowed herself to *feel*, to dare to connect with another human being after the hell she'd suffered with her mother.

She was in no danger of forgetting; if she did, she had the tattoo on her shoulder to remind her.

Sakis pressed the 'end' button on yet another phone call and leaned back against the club seat's head-rest.

Across from him, the tap-tap of the keyboard filled the silence as his assistant worked away at the ever-growing list of tasks he'd been throwing at her since they'd taken off four hours ago.

Turning his head, he glanced at her. As usual her face was expressionless save the occasional crease at the corner of her eyes as she squinted at the screen. Her brow remained smooth and untroubled as her fingers flew over the keyboard.

Her sleek blonde hair was in the same pristine, precise knot it had been when she'd arrived at work at six o'clock this morning. Without conscious thought, his gaze traced over her, again feeling that immediate zing to his senses.

Her dress suit was impeccable—a black-and-white combination that looked a bit severe but suited her perfectly. In her lobes, pearl earrings gleamed, small and unassuming.

His gaze slid down her neck, past slim shoulders and over the rest of her body, examining her in a way he rarely permitted himself to. The sight of the gentle curve of her breasts, her flat stomach and her long, shapely legs made his hands flex on his armrests as the zing turned stronger.

Moneypenny was fit, if a little on the slim side. Despite his slave-driving schedule, not once in the last year and a half had she turned up late for work or called in sick. He knew she stayed in the executive apartment in Pantelides Towers more and more lately rather than return to… He frowned. To wherever it was she called home.

Again he thanked whatever deity had sent her his way.

After his hellish experience with his last executive assistant, Giselle, he'd seriously contemplated commissioning a robot to handle his day-to-day life. When he'd read Brianna's flawless CV, he'd convinced himself she was too good to be true. He'd only reconsidered her after all the other candidates, after purporting to have almost identical supernatural abilities, had turned up at the interviews with not-so-hidden agendas—ones that involved getting into his bed at the earliest opportunity.

Brianna Moneypenny's file had listed talents that made him wonder why another competitor hadn't snapped her up. No one that good would've been jobless, even in the current economic climate. He'd asked her as much.

Her reply had been simple: 'You're the best at what you do. I want to work for the best.'

His hackles had risen at that response, but there had been no guile, no coquettish lowering of her lashes or strategic crossing of her legs. If anything, she'd looked defiant.

Thinking back now, he realised that was the first time he'd felt it—that tug on his senses that accompanied the electrifying sensation when he looked into her eyes.

Of course, he dismissed the feeling whenever it arose. Feelings had no place in his life or his business.

What he'd wanted was an efficient assistant who could rise to any challenge he set her. Moneypenny had risen to each challenge and continued to surprise him on a regular basis, a rare thing in a man of his position.

His gaze finally reached her feet and, with a sharp dart of astonishment, he noted the tiny tattoo on the inside of her left ankle. The star-shaped design, its circumference no larger than his thumb, was inked in black and blue and stood out against her pale skin.

Although he was staring straight at it, the mark

was so out of sync with the rest of her no-nonsense persona, he wondered if he was hallucinating.

No, it was definitely a tattoo, right there, etched into her flawless skin.

Intrigued, he returned his gaze to the busy fingers tapping away. As if sensing his scrutiny, her fingers slowed and her head started to lift and turn towards him.

Sakis glanced down at his watch. 'We'll be landing in three hours. Let's take a break now and regroup in half an hour.'

Despite the loud whirr of her laptop shutting down, he noticed her attention didn't stray far from the device. Her attention never wavered from her work—a fact that should've pleased him.

'I've ordered lunch to be served in five minutes. I can hold it off for a few more minutes if you would like to look over the bios of the people we need to speak to when we land?' Her gaze met his, her blue eyes cool and unwavering.

His gaze dropped again to her ankle. As he watched, she slowly re-crossed her legs, obscuring the tattoo from his gaze.

'Mr Pantelides?' came the cool query.

Sakis inhaled slowly, willed his wavering control to slide back into place. By the time his gaze reconnected with hers, his interest in her tattoo had receded to the back of his mind.

*Receded, but not been obliterated.*

'Have lunch served in ten. I'll go take a quick shower.' He rose and headed for the larger of the two bedrooms at the rear of his plane.

At the door, he glanced back over his shoulder. Brianna Moneypenny was reaching for the attendant intercom with one hand while reopening her laptop with the other.

Super-efficient and ultra-professional. His executive assistant was everything she'd said on the tin, just like he'd explained to Ari.

But it suddenly occurred to Sakis that, in the eighteen months she'd worked for him, he'd never bothered looking *inside* the tin.

# CHAPTER TWO

'I NEED TO get to the site asap once we land,' Sakis said in between bites of his chef-made gourmet beef burger.

Brianna curbed her pang of envy as she forked her plain, low-fat, crouton-free salad *niçoise* into her mouth and shook her head. 'The environment minister wants a meeting first. I tried to postpone it but he was insistent. I think he wants a photo op, this being an election year and all. I told him it'd have to be a brief meeting.'

His jaw tightened on his bite, his eyes narrowing with displeasure. Brianna didn't have to wonder why.

Sakis Pantelides detested any form of media attention with an almost unholy hatred, courtesy of the public devastation and humiliation Alexandrou Pantelides had visited on his family two decades ago. The Pantelides' downfall had been played out in full media glare.

'I have a helicopter on standby to take you straight to the site when you're done.'

'Make sure his people know my definition of *brief.* Do we know what the media presence is at the site?' he asked after swallowing another mouthful.

Her gaze darted to his. Green eyes watched her like a hawk. 'All the major global networks are present. We also have a couple of EPA ships in the area monitoring things.'

He gave a grim nod. 'There's not much we can do about the Environmental Protection Agency's presence, but make sure security know that they can't be allowed to interfere in the salvage and clean-up process. Rescuing the wildlife and keeping pollution to a minimum is another top priority.'

'I know. And...I had an idea.' Her plan was risky, in that it could attract more media attention than Sakis would agree to, but if she managed to pull it off it would reap enormous benefits and buy back some goodwill for Pantelides Shipping. It would also cement her invaluable status in Sakis's eyes and she could finally be rid of the sinking, rock-hard feeling in her stomach when she woke in a cold sweat many nights.

Some might find it shallow but Brianna placed job security above everything else. After everything she'd been through as a child—naively trusting that the only parent she had would put her well-being ahead of the clamour of the next drug fix—keeping her job and her small Docklands apartment meant everything to her. The terror of not knowing where her next meal would come from or when her temporary home would be taken from her still haunted her. And after her foolish decision to risk giving her trust, and the steep price she'd paid for it, she'd vowed never to be that helpless again.

'Moneypenny, I'm listening,' Sakis said briskly, and she realised he was waiting for her to speak.

Gathering her fracturing thoughts, she took a deep breath.

'I was thinking we can use the media and social network sites to our advantage. A few environmental blogs have started up, and they're comparing what's happening with the other oil conglomerate incident a few years ago. We need to nip that in the bud before it gets out of hand.'

Sakis frowned. 'It isn't even remotely the same thing. For one thing, this is a surface spill, not a deep sea pipeline breach.'

'But…'

His expression turned icy. 'I'd also like to keep the media out of this as much as possible. Things tend to get twisted around when the media becomes involved.'

'I believe this is the ideal time to bring them round to our side. I know a few journalists who are above-board. Perhaps, if we can work exclusively with them, we can get a great result. We've admitted the error is ours, so there's nothing to cover up. But not everyone has time to fact-check and the public making assumptions could be detrimental to us. We need to keep the line of communication wide open so people know everything that's going on at every stage.'

'What do you propose?' Sakis pushed his plate away.

She followed suit and fired up her laptop. Keying in the address, she called up the page she'd been working on. 'I've started a blog with a corresponding social networking accounts.' She turned the screen towards him and held her breath.

He glanced down at it. '"Save Point Noire"?'

She nodded.

'What is the point of that, exactly?'

'It's an invitation for anyone who wants to volunteer—either physically at the site or online with expertise.'

Sakis started to shake his head and her heart

took a dive. 'Pantelides Shipping is responsible for this. We'll clean up our own mess.'

'Yes, but shutting ourselves off can also cause us a huge negative backlash. Look—' she indicated the numbers on the screen '—we're trending worldwide. People want to get involved.'

'Won't they see it as soliciting free help?'

'Not if we give them something in return.'

His gaze scoured her face, intense and focused, and Brianna felt a tiny burst of heat in her belly. Feverishly, she pushed it away.

'And what would that something be?' he asked.

Nerves suddenly attacked her stomach. 'I haven't thought that far ahead. But I'm sure I can come up with something before the day's out.'

He kept staring at her for so long, her insides churned harder. Reaching for his glass, he took a long sip of water, his gaze still locked on her.

'Just when I think you're out of tricks, you surprise me all over again, Miss Moneypenny.' The slow, almost lazy murmur didn't throw her. What threw her was the keen speculation in his eyes.

Brianna held his gaze even though she yearned to look away. Speculation led to curiosity. Curiosity was something she didn't want to attract from her boss, or anyone for that matter. Her past needed to stay firmly, irretrievably buried.

'I'm not sure I know what you mean, Mr Pantelides.'

He glanced down at the laptop. 'Your plan is ingenious but, while I commend you for its inception, I'm also aware that keeping track of all the information flowing in will be a monumental task. How do you propose to do that?'

'If you give me the go-ahead, I can brief a small team back at the head office to take over. Any relevant information or genuine volunteer will be put through to me and I can take it from there.'

The decisive shake of his head made her want to clench her fist in disappointment. 'I need you with me once we get on site. I can't have you running off to check your emails every few minutes.'

'I can ask for three-hourly email updates.' When his gaze remained sceptical, she rushed on. 'You said so yourself—it's a great idea. At least let me have a go at trying to execute it. We need the flow of information now more than ever and getting the public on our side can't hurt. What do we have to lose?'

After a minute, he nodded. 'Four-hourly updates. But we make cleaning up the spill our top priority.'

'Of course.' She reached for the laptop but he leaned forward, took it from her and set it down beside his plate.

'Leave that for now. You haven't finished your meal.'

Surprised, she glanced down at her half-finished plate. 'Um…I sort of had.'

He pushed her plate towards her. 'You'll need your strength for what's ahead. Eat.'

Her gaze slid to his own unfinished meal as she picked up her fork. 'What about you?'

'My stamina is much more robust than yours—no offence.'

'None taken at all.' Her voice emerged a little stiffer than she intended.

Sakis quirked one eyebrow. 'Your response is at variance with your tone, Miss Moneypenny. I'm sure some die-hard feminist would accuse me of being sexist, but you really need it more than I do. You barely eat enough as it is.'

She gripped her fork harder. 'I wasn't aware my diet was under scrutiny.'

'It's hard to miss that you watch what you eat with almost military precision. If it wasn't absurd, I'd think you were rationing yourself.' His eyes were narrowed in that unnervingly probing way.

Her pulse skittered in alarm at the observation. 'Maybe I am.'

His lips tightened. 'Well, going without food for the sake of vanity is dangerous. You're risking your health, and thereby your ability to function properly. It's your duty to ensure you're in the right shape so you can fulfil your duties.'

The vehemence in his tone made her alarm escalate. 'Why do I get the feeling we're talking about more than my abandoned salad?'

He didn't answer immediately. His lowered lids and closed expression told her the memory wasn't a pleasant one.

He settled back in his seat, outwardly calm. But Brianna saw the hand still wrapped around his water glass wasn't quite so steady. 'Watching someone wilfully waste away despite being surrounded by abundance isn't exactly a forgettable experience.'

Her grip went slack. 'I'm sorry…I didn't mean to dredge up bad memories for you. Who do you…?'

He shook his head once and indicated her plate. 'It doesn't matter. Don't let your food go to waste, Moneypenny.'

Brianna glanced down at the remnants of her meal, trying to reconcile the outwardly confident man sitting across from her with the man whose hands trembled at a deeply disturbing memory. Not that she'd even been foolish enough to think Sakis Pantelides was one-faceted.

She recalled that one moment during her interview when he'd looked up from her file, his green eyes granite-hard and merciless.

'If you are to survive this job, I'd strongly urge you to take one piece of advice, Miss Moneypenny. Don't fall in love with me.'

Her response had been quick, painful memory making her tongue acid-sharp. 'With respect, Mr Pantelides, I'm here for the salary. The benefits package isn't too bad either, but most of all I'm here for the top-notch experience. To my knowledge, love never has and never will pay the bills.'

What she'd wanted to add then was that she'd been there, done her time and had the tattoo to prove it.

What she wanted tell him now was that she'd endured far, far worse than a hungry stomach. That she'd known the complete desolation of coming a poor second to her mother's love for drugs. She'd slept rougher than any child deserved to and had fought every day to survive in a concrete jungle, surrounded by the drug-addled bullies with vicious fists.

She held her tongue because to speak would be to reveal far more than she could ever afford to reveal.

Curiosity gnawed at her but she refused to probe further. Probing would invite reciprocity. Her past was under lock and key, tucked behind a titanium vault and sealed in concrete. And that was exactly where she intended to keep it.

In silence, she finished her meal and looked up with relief as the attendant arrived to clear away their plates.

When the phone rang, she pounced on it, grabbing the familiarity that came with work in an effort to banish the brief moments of unguarded intimacy.

'The captain of the coast guard is on the line for you.'

Sakis's gaze swept over her face, a speculative gleam in his eyes that slowly disappeared as he took the phone.

With an inward sigh of relief, Brianna reached for her laptop and fired it up.

Sakis's first glimpse of the troubled tanker made his gut clench hard. He tapped the helicopter pilot on the shoulder.

'Circle the vessel, would you? I want to assess the damage from the air before we land.'

The pilot obliged. Sakis's jaw tightened as he grasped the full impact of the damage of the tanker bearing the black and gold Pantelides colours.

He signalled for the pilot to land and alighted

the moment the chopper touched down. A group of scandal-hungry journalists stood behind the cordoned-off area. From painful experience, Moneypenny's suggestion to bring them on-side rankled, but Sakis didn't dismiss the fact that in this instance she was right.

Ignoring them for now, he strode to where the crew waited, dressed in yellow, high-visibility jumpsuits.

'What's the situation?' he asked.

The head of the salvage crew—a thickset, middle-aged man with greying hair—stepped forward. 'We've managed to get inside the tanker and assessed the damage with the investigation team—we have three breached compartments. The other compartments haven't been affected but, the longer the vessel stays askew, the more likely we are to have another breach. We're working as fast as we can to set up the pumps to drain the compartment and the spillage.'

'How long will it take?'

'Thirty-six to forty-eight hours. Once the last of the crew get here, we'll work around the clock.'

Sakis nodded and turned to see Brianna emerge from the hastily set-up tents on the far side of the beach. For a moment he couldn't reconcile the woman heading towards him with his usual impeccably dressed assistant. Not that she had a hair out of place, of course. But she'd changed into cargo pants and a white T-shirt which was neatly tucked in and belted tight, emphasising her trim waist. Her shining hair made even more vivid by the fierce African sun was still caught in an immaculate knot, but on her feet she wore weathered combat boots.

For the second time today, Sakis felt the attraction he'd ruthlessly battened down strain at the leash.

Ignoring it, he turned his attention to the man next to him. 'It'll be nightfall in three hours. How many boats do you have conducting the search?'

'We have four boats, including the two you provided. Your helicopter is also assisting with the search.' The captain wiped a trickle of sweat off his face. 'But what worries me is the possibility of pirates.'

His gut clenched. 'You think they've been kidnapped?'

The captain nodded. 'We can't rule it out.'

Brianna's eyes widened, then she extracted her mini-tablet from her thigh pocket, her fingers flying over the keypad.

One corner of her lower lip was caught between her teeth as she pressed buttons. A small spike of heat broke through the tight anxiety in his gut. Without giving it the tiniest room, Sakis smashed down on it. *Hard.*

'What is it, Moneypenny?' he asked briskly after he'd dismissed the captain.

Her brow creased but she didn't look up. 'I'm sorry, I should've anticipated the pirates angle...'

He caught her chin with his forefinger and gently forced her head up. When her gaze connected with his, he saw the trace of distress in her eyes.

'That's what the investigators are here for. Besides, you've had a lot to deal with in the last several hours. What I need is the list of journalists you promised. Can you handle that?'

Her nod made her skin slide against his finger. Soft. Silky. Smooth.

*Stási!*

He stepped back abruptly and pushed the aberration from his mind.

Turning, he moved towards the shoreline, conscious that she'd fallen into step beside him. From the air, he'd guestimated that the oil had spread about half a mile along the shore. As he surveyed the frantic activity up and down the once pristine shoreline, regret bit deep.

Whatever had triggered this accident, the blame for the now-blackened, polluted water lay with him, just as he was responsible for the missing crew members. Whatever it took, he would make this right.

The captain of the salvage crew brought the small boat near and Sakis went towards it. When Brianna moved towards him, he shook his head.

'No, stay here. This could be dangerous.'

She frowned. 'If you're going aboard the tanker, you'll need someone to jot down the details and take pictures of the damage.'

'I merely want to see the damage from the inside myself. I'm leaving everything else in the hands of the investigators. And, if I need to, I'm sure I can handle taking a few pictures. What I'm not sure of is the situation inside the vessel and I won't risk you getting injured under any circumstances.' He held out his hand for the camera slung around her neck.

She looked ready to argue with him. Beneath her T-shirt, her chest rose and fell as she exhaled and Sakis forced himself not to glance down as another spike of erotic heat lanced his groin.

*Theos…*

The unsettling feeling made him snap his fingers, an irritatingly frantic need to step away from her charging into him.

'If you're sure,' she started.

'I'm sure.'

By the time she freed herself from the camera strap and handed it over, her face had settled once more into its customary serene professionalism.

Her fingers brushed his as he took the camera and Sakis registered a single instance of softness before the contact was disconnected.

Taking a deep breath, he started to walk away.

'Wait!'

He turned back. 'What is it, Moneypenny?' His tone was harsh but couldn't stop the disturbing edginess creeping over him.

She held out a large yellow jumpsuit. 'You can't get on the boat without wearing this. The health and safety guidelines require it.'

Despite the grim situation, Sakis wanted to laugh at her implacable expression as she held him to account.

'Then by all means…if the guidelines require it.'

He took the plastic garment, shook it out and stepped into it under her watchful eye. He glanced at her as he zipped the jumpsuit and once again saw her lower lip caught between her teeth.

With more force than was necessary, he shoved the small digital camera into the waterproof pocket and trudged through the oil-slicked water.

An hour later, the words of his lead investigator made his heart sink.

'I retired from piloting tankers like these ten years ago, and even then the navigation systems were state-of-the-art. Your vessel has the best one I've ever seen. There's no way this was systems failure. Too many fail-safes in place for the vessel to veer this far off course.'

Sakis gave a grim nod and pulled his phone from his pocket. 'Moneypenny, get me the head of security. I want to know everything about Morgan Lowell… Yes, the captain of my tanker. And prepare a press release. Unfortunately, the investigators are almost certain this was pilot error.'

Brianna perused the electronic page for typos. Once she was satisfied, she approached where Sakis stood with the environment minister. His yellow jumpsuit was unzipped to the waist, displaying the dark-green T-shirt that moulded his lean, sleekly muscular torso. She'd never thought she'd find the sight of a man slipping on a hideous yellow jumpsuit so…hot and unsettling.

He turned, and she held her breath as his gaze swept over her. The crackle of electricity she'd felt earlier when their fingers had touched returned.

Abruptly she pushed it away. They were caught

in a severely fraught set of circumstances. What she was experiencing was just residual adrenaline that came with these unfortunate events.

'Is it ready?' he asked.

She nodded and passed the press release over, along with the list of names he'd requested. He skimmed the words then passed the tablet back to her. Brianna knew he'd memorised every single word.

'I'll go and prep the media.'

She headed for the group of journalists poised behind the white cordon. As she walked, she practised the breathing exercises she'd mastered long before she'd come to work for Sakis Pantelides.

By the time she reached the group, she'd calmed her roiling emotions.

'Good evening, ladies and gentlemen. This is how it's going to work. Mr Pantelides will give his statement. Then he'll invite questions—one from each of you.' She held out a hand at the immediate protests. 'I'm sure you'll understand that it'll take hours for every question you've jotted down to be answered and frankly we don't have time for that. Right now the priority is the salvage operation. So, one question each.' Control settled over her as her steely gaze held the group's and received their cooperation.

*Yes, that was more like it.* Not for her the searing, jittery feelings of the last few hours, ever since she'd looked up on the plane and caught Sakis's gaze on her ankle tattoo; since he'd touched her on the beach, told her not to worry that she'd missed the pirates angle. Those few minutes had been intensely…*rattling.*

The momentary heat she'd seen in his eyes had thrown her off-balance. At the start of her employment she'd taken pains to hide the tattoo but, after realising Sakis took no notice of what she wore or anything about her, she'd relaxed. The sensation of his eyes on her tattoo had smashed a fist through her tight control.

It had taken hours to restore it but, now she had, she was determined not to lose it again.

There was too much at stake.

Feeling utterly composed, she glanced over to where Sakis waited at the assembled podium. At his nod, she signalled security to let the media through.

She stood next to the podium and tried not to let his deep voice affect her as he started speaking. His authority and confidence as he outlined the plans for the salvage mission and the search for the missing crew belied the tension in his body. From her position, she could see the rigid outline of his washboard stomach and the braced tension in his legs. Even though his hands remained loose at his sides, his shoulders barely moved as he spoke.

A camera flashed nearby and she saw his tiniest flinch.

'What's going to happen to the remaining oil on board?' a reporter asked.

His gaze swung to where the minister stood. 'For their very generous assistance, we're donating the contents on board the distressed vessel to the coast guard and army. The minister has kindly offered to co-ordinate the distribution.'

'So you're just going to give away oil worth millions of dollars, out of the goodness of your heart? Are you trying to bribe your way out of your company's responsibilities, Mr Pantelides?'

Brianna's breath stalled but Sakis barely blinked at the caustic remark from a particularly vile tabloid reporter. That he didn't visibly react was a testament to his unshakeable control.

'On the contrary, as I said at the start, my company assumes one hundred per cent liability for this incident and are working with the government in making reparations. No price is too high to pay for ensuring that the clean-up process is speedy and causes minimum damage to the sea life. This means the remaining crude oil has to be removed as quickly as possible and the vessel secured and towed away. Rather than transfer it to another Pantelides tanker, a process that'll take time, I've decided to donate it to the government. I'm sure you'll agree it makes perfect sense.' His tone remained even but the tic in his jaw belied his simmering anger. 'Next question.'

'Can you confirm what caused the accident? According to your sources, this is one of your newest tankers, equipped with state-of-the-art navigation systems, so what went wrong?'

'That is a question for our investigators to answer once they'd finished their work.'

'What does your gut feeling say?'

'I choose to rely on hard facts when stakes are this high, not gut feelings,' Sakis responded, his tone clipped.

'You haven't made a secret of your dislike for the media. Are you going to use that to try and stop the media from reporting on this accident, Mr Pantelides?'

'You wouldn't be here if I felt that way. In fact—' he stopped and flicked a glance at Brianna before facing the crowd, but not before she caught a glimpse of the banked unease in his eyes '—I've hand-picked five journalists who will be given exclusive access to the salvage process.'

He read out the names. While the chosen few preened, the rest of the media erupted with shouted questions.

One in particular filtered through. 'If your father were alive and in your place, how would he react to this incident? Would he try and buy his way out of it, like he did with everything else?'

The distressed sound slipped from Brianna's throat before she could stop it. Silence fell over the gathered group as the words froze in the air. Beneath the podium, out of sight of the media's glare, Sakis's hands clenched into white-knuckled fists.

The urge to protect him surged out of nowhere and swept over her in an overwhelming wave. Her heart lurched, bringing with it a light-headedness that made her sway where she stood. Sakis's quick sideways glance told her he'd noticed.

Facing the media, he inhaled slowly. 'You have to go to the afterlife to ask my father that question. I do not speak for the dead.'

He stepped from the podium and stood directly in front of her. The breadth of his broad shoulders blocked out the sun.

'What's wrong?' he demanded in a fierce whisper.

'N...nothing. Everything is fine.... Going according to plan.' She fought to maintain her steady breathing even as she flailed inside. Needing desperately to claw back her control, she searched blindly for the solid reassurance of her mini-tablet.

Sakis plucked it out of her hands, his piercing gaze unwavering as it remained trained on her. '*According to plan* would be these damned vultures finding another carcass to pick on and leaving us to get on with the work that needs to be done.' From his tone, there was no sign that the last question had had a lasting effect on him, but this close she saw his pinched lips and the ruthlessly suppressed pain in his eyes. Another wave of protectiveness rushed over her.

*Purpose*. That was what she needed. Purpose and focus.

Swallowing hard, she held out her hand for her tablet. 'I'll take care of it. You've chosen the journalists you want to cover the salvage operation. There's no need for the rest to hang around.'

He didn't relinquish it. 'Are you sure you're all right? You look pale. I hope you're not succumbing to the heat. Have you had anything to eat since we got here?'

'I'm fine, Mr Pantelides.' He kept staring at her, dark brows clamped in a frown. 'I assure you, there's nothing wrong.' She deliberately made her voice crisp. 'The sooner I get rid of the media, the sooner we can get on with things.'

He finally let her take the tablet from him. Hardly daring to breathe, Brianna stepped back and away from the imposing man in front of her.

*No. No. No...*

The negative sound reverberated through her skull as she walked away. There was no way she was developing feelings for her boss.

Even if Sakis didn't fire her the moment she betrayed even the slightest non-professional emotion, she had no intention of letting herself down like that ever again.

The tattoo on her ankle throbbed.

The larger one on her shoulder burned with the fierce reminder.

She'd spent two years in jail for her serious error in judgement after funnelling her need to be loved towards the wrong guy.

Making the same mistake again was not an option.

# CHAPTER THREE

SAKIS WATCHED BRIANNA walk away; her back was held so rigid her upper half barely moved. His frown deepened. Something was wrong. Granted, this was the first crisis they'd been thrown into together, but her conduct up till now had been beyond exemplary.

Right up until she'd reacted strongly to the journalist's question. A question he himself had not anticipated. He should've known that somehow his father would be dredged up like this. Should've known that, even from beyond the grave, the parent who'd held his family in such low, deplorable regard would not remain buried. He stomped on the pain riding just beneath his chest, the way he always did when he thought of his father. He refused to let the past haunt him. It no longer had any power over him.

After what his father had done to his family, to his mother especially, he deserved to be forgotten totally and utterly.

Unfortunately, at times like these, when the media thought they could get a whiff of scandal, they pounced. And this time, there was no escaping their rabid focus…

The deafening sound of the industrial-size vacuum starting up drew his attention from Brianna, reminding him that he had more important things to deal with than his hitherto unruffled personal assistant's off behaviour, and the unwanted memories of a ghost.

He zipped his jumpsuit back up and strode over to the black, slick shoreline. Half a mile away, giant oil-absorbing booms floated around the perimeter of the contaminated water to catch the spreading spill. Closer to shore, right in the middle of where the oil poured out, ecologically safe chemicals pumped from huge sprays to dissolve as much of the slick as possible.

*It's not enough.* It would never be enough because this shouldn't have happened in the first place.

His phone rang and he recognised Theo's number on his screen.

'What's happening, brother? Talk to me,' Theo said.

Sakis summarised the situation as quickly as he could, leaving out nothing, even though he was very aware that the mention of kidnap would raise painful, unwanted memories for Theo.

'Anything I can do from here?' his brother asked. The only hint of his disturbance at being reminded of his own kidnap when he was eighteen was the slight ring of steel in his voice when he asked the question. 'I can put you in touch with the right people if you want. I made it my business to find out who the right contacts are in a situation like this.' His analytical brain wouldn't have made him cope with his ordeal otherwise.

That was Theo through and through. He went after a problem until he had every imaginable scenario broken down, then he went after the solution with single-minded determination—which was why he fulfilled his role as trouble-shooter for Pantelides Inc so perfectly.

'We've got it in hand. But perhaps you could cause an outrageous scandal where you are, distract these damned paparazzi from messing with my salvage operation.'

'Hmm, I suppose I could skydive naked from the top of *Cristo Redentor*,' Theo offered.

For the first time in what felt like days, Sakis's lips cracked in a smile. 'You love Rio too much to get yourself barred from the city for ever for blasphemy.' His gaze flicked to where Brianna stood alone, having dispersed the last of the journalists. She was back on her tablet, her fingers busy on the glass keyboard.

Satisfaction oozed through him. Whatever had fractured his PA's normal efficiency, she had it back again.

'Everything's in hand,' he repeated, probably more to reassure himself that he had his emotions under control.

'Great to hear. Keep me in the loop, *ne*?'

Sakis signed off and jumped into the nearest boat carrying a crew of six and the vacuum, and signalled to the pilot to head out.

For the next three hours, while sunlight prevailed, he worked with the crew to pump as much sludge of out the water as possible. From another boat nearby, the journalists to whom he'd granted access filmed the process. Some even asked intelligent questions that didn't make his teeth grind.

Floodlights arrived, mounted on tripods on more boats, and he carried on working.

It was nearing midnight when, alerted to the arrival of the refresh crew, he straightened from where he'd been managing the pump. And froze.

'*What the hell?*'

The salvage-crew captain glanced up sharply. 'Excuse me, sir?'

But Sakis's gaze was on the boat about twenty yards to his left, where Brianna held the nozzle of a chemical spray aimed at the slick, a distressed look on her face as she swung her arm back and forth over the water.

The first of the changeover crew was approaching on a motor-powered dinghy. Sakis hopped into the small vessel and directed it to where Brianna worked.

Seeing him approach on a direct course, she changed the angle of her nozzle to avoid spraying him, her face hurriedly set in its usual calm expression. It was almost as if the bleakness he'd glimpsed moments ago had been a mirage.

'Mr Pantelides, did you need something?'

For some reason, the sound of his father's name on her lips aggravated him. For several hours he'd managed not to think about his father. He wanted to keep it that way. 'Put that hose down and get in.'

She turned the spray off, eyes widening. 'Excuse me?'

'Get in here. *Now*.'

'I...I don't understand,' she said. Her voice had lost a little of the sharpness and she looked genuinely puzzled as she stared down at him.

He saw the long streak of oil across her cheek. Her once white T-shirt had now turned grimy and slick and her khaki cargo pants had suffered the same fate.

But not a single hair was out of place.

The dichotomy of dirt, flawless efficiency and the bleakness he'd glimpsed a moment ago intrigued him beyond definition. The intrigue escalated his irritation. 'It's almost midnight. You should've left here hours ago.' He manoeuvred the dinghy until it bumped the boat, directly below where she stood on the starboard side.

From that angle, he couldn't miss the landscape of her upper body—more specifically, the perfect shape of her breasts or the sleek line of her jaw and neck as she glanced down at him.

'Oh. Well…I'm here to work, Mr Pantelides. Why should I have left?'

'Because you're not part of the salvage team, and even they work in six-hour shifts. Besides this—' he waved at the nozzle in her hand '—is not part of your job description.'

'I'm aware of what my job description is. But, if we're being pedantic, you're not part of the crew either. And yet here you are.'

Sakis felt a shake of surprise. In all her time with him, she'd never raised her voice or shown signs of feminine ire. But in the last few minutes, he'd seen intense emotion ream over her face and through her voice. Right now, Sakis had the distinct feeling she was extremely displeased with his directive. A small spurt of masochistic pleasure fizzed through him at the thought that he'd unruffled the unflappable Miss Moneypenny.

'I'm the boss. I have the luxury of doing whatever the hell I want,' he said softly, his gaze raking her face, secretly eager for further animated reaction.

What he got was unexpected. Her shoulders slumped and she shrugged. 'Of course. But, just in case you're worried about the corporate risks, I signed a waiver before coming aboard. So you'll suffer no liability if anything happens to me.'

Irritation returned, bit deeper. 'I don't give a damn about personal liability or corporate risks. What I do give a damn about is your ability to function properly tomorrow if you don't get enough sleep. You've been up for over eighteen hours. So, unless you have super powers I'm not aware of, put that hose down and get down here.' He held out a hand, unwilling to examine this almost clawing need to take care of her.

She didn't put the hose down. Instead she handed it over to a salvage crew member. Finally, she faced Sakis.

'Fine. You win.' Again he saw the tiniest mutinous set to her lips and wondered why that little action pleased him so much.

He was tired; he *must* be hallucinating. He certainly wasn't thinking straight if the thought of getting under his executive assistant's skin held so much of his interest.

She swung long, slim legs over the side of the boat and dropped into the dinghy. The movement made the vessel sway. She swayed with it, and threw out a hand to steady herself as Sakis turned.

Her torso bumped his arm and her hand landed on his shoulder as she tried to find her feet. His arm snagged her waist, encountered firm, warm muscle beneath his fingers.

Heat punched through his chest and arrowed straight for his groin.

'*Stasi!*'

'I...I'm sorry,' she stammered, pulling away with a skittishness very unlike her.

'No harm done,' he murmured. But Sakis wasn't so hot on that reassurance. Harm was being done to his insides. Heat continued to ravage him, firing sensations he sure as hell didn't want fired up. And especially not with his PA.

A quick glance showed she'd retreated to the farthest part of the small dinghy with her arms crossed primly around her middle and her face averted from his. He tried not to let his gaze drop to her plump breasts…but, *Theos*, it was hard not to notice their tempting fullness.

With a muttered curse, his hand tightened on the rudder of the dinghy and steered it towards shore.

This time she didn't refuse his offer of help when they stepped into the shallow water. After making sure the vessel was secure, he followed her onto the floodlit beach.

When he neared, he caught another glimpse of distress on her face.

'What's wrong? Why were you on the salvage boat? And, before you trot out "nothing", I'd advise you not to insult my intelligence.'

He saw her hesitate, then shove her hands into her pockets. This time, he couldn't stop himself from staring at her chest. Thankfully, she didn't notice because her gaze wasn't on him.

'I was talking to the some of the locals earlier. This cove was a special place for them, a sanctuary. I…I felt bad about what's happened.'

Guilt lanced through him. But, more than that, the rare glimpse into Brianna Moneypenny's human side intrigued him more than ever. 'I'll make sure it's returned to them as pristine as it once was.'

Her gaze flew up and connected with his, surprise and pleasure reflected in her eyes. 'That's good. It's not nice when your sanctuary is ripped away from you.' The pain accompanying those words made him frown. Before he could probe deeper, she stepped back. 'Anyway, I assured them you would make it right.'

'Thank you.'

She started to walk towards the fleet of four-wheelers a short distance away. Their driver stood next to the first one.

'I reserved a suite for you at the Noire. Your case was taken there a few hours ago and your laptop and phones are in the jeep. I'll see you in the morning, Mr Pantelides,' she tagged on.

Sakis froze. '*You'll see me in the morning?* Aren't you coming with me?'

'No,' she said.

'Why not?'

'Because I'm not staying at the hotel.'

'Where exactly are you staying?'

She indicated the double row of yellow tents set up further up on the beach, away from the bustle of the clean-up work.

'I've secured a tent and put my stuff in there.'

'What's wrong with staying at the same hotel I'm staying in?'

'Nothing, except they didn't have any more

rooms. The suite I reserved for you was the last one. The other hotels are too far away to make the commute efficient.'

Sakis shook his head. 'You've been on your feet all day with barely a break— Don't argue with me, Moneypenny,' He raised a hand when she started to speak. 'You're not sleeping in a flimsy tent on the beach with machines blasting away all around you. Go and get your things.'

'I assure you, it's more than adequate.'

'No. You say I have a suite?'

'Yes.'

'Then there is no reason why we can't share it.'

'I would rather not, Mr Pantelides.'

The outright refusal shocked and annoyed him in equal measures. Also another first from Brianna Moneypenny was the fact that she wasn't quite meeting his gaze. 'Why would you *rather not*?'

She hesitated.

'Look at me, Moneypenny,' he commanded.

Blue eyes… No, they weren't quite blue. They were a shade of aquamarine, wide, lushly lashed and beautiful…and they met his in frank challenge. 'Your room is a single suite with one double bed. It's not suitable for two, um, professionals, and I'd rather not have to share my personal space.'

Sakis thought of the countless women who

would jump at the chance to share 'personal space' with him.

He thought of all the women who would kill to share a double bed with him.

Then he thought of why he was here, in this place: with *his* oil contaminating a once incredibly beautiful beach; *his* crew missing; and the tabloid press just waiting for him to slip up, to show them that the apple hadn't fallen far from the tree.

The sick feeling that he'd forced down but never quite suppressed enough threatened to rise again. It was the same mingled despair and anger he'd felt when Theo had been taken. The same sense of helplessness when he'd been unable to do anything to stop his mother fading away before his eyes, her pain raw and wrenching after what his father and the media had done to her.

'I don't give a damn about your personal space. What I do give a damn about is your ability to fire on all cylinders. We discussed this—you being up to standing by me in this situation we find ourselves in. You assured me you were up to the task. And yet, for the last ten minutes, you've shown a certain…mutiny that makes me wonder whether you're equipped to handle what's coming.'

Her outrage made her breathing erratic. 'I don't think that's a fair observation, sir. I've done everything you've asked of me, and I'm more than capable of handling whatever comes. Just because I disagree with you on one small issue doesn't make me mutinous. I'm thinking about you.'

'Then prove it. Stop arguing with me and get in the jeep.'

She opened her mouth; closed it again. When she looked at him, her eyes held a hint of fire he'd seen more than once today. The fire *he'd* tried—and failed—to bank fired up deep in his groin.

'I'll go and get my things,' she said.

'No need.' He exchanged glances with the driver and the young man headed towards the row of tents. Sakis leaned against the jeep's hood. 'You can fill me in on the results of your social media campaign while we wait.'

He saw how eagerly she snatched at her tablet and suppressed another bout of irritation. Whatever was causing this abnormal behaviour, he needed to nip it in the bud pretty darned quick. The crisis on his hands needed all his attention.

'I've found six individuals who I think will be useful to us. One's a professor of marine biology based in Guinea Bissau. Another, a husband and wife team who are experts in wildlife rescue. They specialise in disaster rescue such as this. The other three have no specialities but they have a huge social media following and are known for volunteering on humanitarian missions. I'm having all six vetted by our security team. If they pass the security test, I'll arrange for them to be flown over tomorrow.'

'I'm still not convinced bringing even more focus on this crisis is the best way to go, Moneypenny.' His insides tightened as he thought of his mother. 'Sometimes you don't see the harm until it's too late.' He thought of her devastation and misery, the incessant sobbing, and finally the substitution of food with alcohol when it'd hit home that the husband she'd thought was a god amongst men, the man she'd thought was true to her and only her, had had a string of affairs with mistresses around the globe, some of whom had dated back to before he'd put his wedding ring on her finger.

The year he'd turned fifteen had been the bleakest year of his life. It was the year he'd had every child's basest fear confirmed—that his father did not love him, did not love anyone or anything but himself. It was also the start of Sakis's hatred of the media, who'd not only exposed his worst fears but trumpeted it to the world.

Ari had withstood the invasion of their lives with his usual unflappable demeanour, although Sakis had a feeling his brother had been just as devastated, if not more so, than he had been. Theo, thirteen at that time, with fresh teenage hormones battering him, had gone off the rails. To this day, their mother had never found out how many times Theo had run away from home because Ari, seventeen going on seventy, had found him every single time and brought him back.

In all that chaos, Sakis had watched his mother deteriorate before his eyes, culminating in her seeking a solution so horrific, he still shuddered at the memory.

He pushed the events of decades past out of his mind and focused on the woman in front of him, who watched him with barely veiled curiosity.

Silently, he held her gaze until hers fell away. That he immediately wished it back made him suppress a frustrated growl.

'The journalists we hand-picked know this could be the opportunity of a lifetime for them as long as they play ball. I'll make sure they portray an open and honest account of what we're doing to remedy the situation, while infusing the appropriate rhetoric to protect the company's reputation.'

A smile tugged at his mouth. 'You should've been a diplomat, Moneypenny.'

Her shoulder lifted in a shrug that drew his attention to where it had no business being, specifically the pulse beating beneath her flawless skin.

'We all have something we desire more than anything. Wasting the opportunity when it presents itself is plain foolishness.'

The temptation to look inside the tin was too much to pass up. 'And what is it *you* want?'

Her startled gaze flew to his. 'Excuse me?'

'What do you want more than anything?'

She shook her head and looked away, a hint of desperation in the movement. He saw her relieved expression as his driver approached, her small carry-all in his hand.

Striding forward, she took the case from the surprised driver and stowed it in the boot. Then she opened the back door and got in.

Sakis took his time to walk to the other door. He ignored her nervous glance and waited until they were both buckled in and the jeep was moving along the dusty road running alongside the beach. The moment she relaxed, he pounced. 'Well?'

'Well what?'

'I'm waiting for an answer.'

'About what I want?' she asked.

Her stall tactics didn't go unnoticed. 'Yes,' he pressed.

'I…want the chance to prove that I can do a good job and be recognised for it.'

He exhaled impatiently. 'You already do an exemplary job, and you're highly paid and highly valued for it.'

He battled the disappointment rising inside. He'd wanted *personal.* From the assistant he'd warned against getting personal. So what? Finding out a little bit about what went on behind that professional façade didn't mean either of them risked losing their highly functional relationship. Besides, Moneypenny knew of his liaisons; she arranged the lunches, dinners and the odd, discreet parting gift.

The balance needed adjusting, just a little. 'Do you have a boyfriend?'

Her head whipped round, perfect eyebrows arching. 'I beg your pardon?'

'It's a very simple question, Moneypenny. One that demands a simple yes or no answer.'

'I know it is, but I fail to see how that's *relevant* within the realms of our working relationship.'

He noted the agitated cadence of her breathing and hid a smile. 'I believe it's company policy to have a yearly appraisal. You've been working for me for almost eighteen months and you're yet to have your first appraisal.'

'HR gave me my appraisal six months ago. They sent you the results, I believe.'

'Probably, but I haven't read it yet.'

'So you want to do your own evaluation…*now*?'

He shrugged, a little irritated with himself now that he was pushing the subject. But, now the question was out there, it niggled and, yes, he wanted to know if Brianna Moneypenny had urges just like the rest of the human race. She wasn't a robot. She'd felt warm and most definitely feminine when her body had brushed against his on the boat. Her comment about restoring the beach for the local inhabitants had also uncovered a hitherto hidden soft side he hadn't expected.

Moneypenny was human. And compassionate. And he was curious about her.

He shifted to ease the sudden restless throb in his body. 'Call it a mini-appraisal. I just want to know if anything on your CV has changed since you joined me. You listed your marital status as single when I employed you. I merely want to know if that's changed in any significant way.'

'So you want to know, purely from a professional point of view, whether I'm sleeping with anyone or not?' Her tone dripped cynicism. 'Do you want to know which brand of underwear I prefer and what I like for breakfast as well?

Sakis felt no shame. *Redressing the balance.* Plus he needed something to take his mind off what had been a hellish day…if only for a moment. 'Yes to my first question; the other two are optional.'

Brianna's chin lifted. 'In that case, since it's for *purely professional* purposes, no, I don't have a lover, my underwear is my own business and I have an unhealthy weakness for pancakes. Are you satisfied?'

The thrill of gratification that arrowed through him made his pulse race dangerously. Disturbingly.

He glanced at the tight coil of golden hair that gleamed as they passed under bright streetlights, at her pert nose and generously wide and full mouth; the dimple that winked in her cheek when she pursed her lips in irritation, like she was doing now…

The thrill escalated, rushing through his blood.

*Theos…*

He rubbed at his tired eyes with the heels of his palms. What the hell was wrong with him? Strong coffee; that was what he needed. Or a stiff drink to knock everything back into perspective.

Because there was no way in hell he planned on following through with this insane attraction to Moneypenny. No damned way…

The streets were deserted as they approached

the leafy centre of Pointe Noire. Their hotel was pleasant enough with a sweeping circular driveway that ended in front of the white three-storey, shutter-windowed pre-colonial building.

The manager waited in the foyer to greet them personally, although his gaze widened when it lit on Brianna.

'Welcome to the Noire, Monsieur Pantelides. Your suite is ready, although I was told you would be the sole occupant?'

'You were misinformed.'

'Ah, well, my apologies for the lack of more prestigious suites but the rooms were all booked up the moment the crash…er…the moment the unfortunate event happened.' He couldn't quite keep the gloating pride from his voice.

As the manager called the lift and they entered the small space, he sensed Brianna's tension mount. The moment they were let into the suite, he understood why.

The 'suite' label had clearly been a lofty idea in someone's deluded mind. The room was only marginally larger than a double room with the sleeping area separated from the double sofa by a TV and drinks unit.

He only half-listened as the manager expounded on the many features of the room. His attention was caught on Brianna, who stood staring at the bed as if it was her mortal enemy, her shoulders stiff and her face even stiffer. Had their whole reason for being here not so dire, he'd have been amused.

He dismissed the manager. He'd barely left when a knock came at the door.

Brianna jumped.

'Relax, it's only our bags,' he reassured her with a frown.

'Oh, yes, of course.'

The porters entered and Sakis made sure they left just as quickly.

Silence reigned, thick and heavy, permeating the air with a sexual atmosphere he recognised but was determined to ignore. It had no business here.

And yet, it refused to be stemmed.

He watched as she came towards him and reached for the bag the porter had left beside him.

'You take the shower first,' he said. The image that slammed into his mind sent a dark tremor through him but he forced himself to breathe through it.

She straightened and her gaze darted to the bathroom door in the so-called suite. 'If you're sure.'

'Yes, I'm sure.' Then, unable to stop himself, even while every sense screamed at him to step away, he reached out and rubbed the smudge on her cheek.

Her breath caught on a strangled gasp, sending another punch of heat through him. His senses screamed harder, but his fingers stayed put, stroking her soft, warm skin.

'You have an oil streak right there.' He rubbed again.

With a sharply drawn breath, she moved away, but her eyes stayed on him, and in their depths Sakis saw the clear evidence of lust…and another emotion he'd never seen in a woman's eyes when it came to him: fear.

*What the hell?*

Before he could question her, she swung away. 'I…I'll try not to take too long.'

With quick strides, she disappeared into the bathroom and slammed the door, leaving him standing there staring at the door with a growing erection and an ever-rising pulse rate that made him certain he risked serious health problems if he didn't get it under control.

*Thee mou…* Of all the times and places—and sheer idiocy, bearing in mind the recipient—it seemed his libido had taken this moment to run rampant and to focus its attention on the one person he should absolutely not focus on.

Crisis heightened the senses and made men and women succumb to inappropriate urges, leading to serious errors of judgment that later came back to bite them in the ass.

Whatever was happening here, he needed to kill it with a swift, merciless death. And he certainly needed not to think of Moneypenny behind that door, removing her clothes, stepping naked, beneath the warm shower…

Moving the drinks cabinet, he poured himself a shot of whiskey. As he downed it, his gaze strayed to the bathroom door.

Nothing was going to happen. He refused to let it.

As if hammering home the point, he heard the distinct sound of the lock sliding home.

And poured himself another drink.

Brianna sagged against the door, unable to catch her breath. The bag slid uselessly from her fingers and she didn't need to look down to see evidence of her body's reaction to Sakis Pantelides. She could feel every inch of her skin tightening, burning, reacting to his touch as if he was still rubbing her cheek.

*No. No. No!*

Anger lent her strength, enough to tug her boots

off and fling them away with distressed disgust. Her oil-smudged cargo pants went the same way, followed by her once white T-shirt. About to reach for the bra clasp, she glanced up and caught the reflection of her tattoo in the wide bathroom mirror.

Sucking in a deep breath, she stepped forward, clutched the sink and struggled to regulate her breathing.

She stared hard at the tattoo on her shoulder. *I refuse to sink.* It was the mantra she'd recited second by second in her darkest days. And one she'd tapped from whenever she needed strength or self-belief...anything to get her through a tough day. It was a reminder of what she'd survived as a child and as an adult. A reminder that depending on anyone for her happiness or wellbeing was asking to be devastated. She'd made that mistake once and look where she'd ended up.

The tattoo was a reminder never to forget. To keep swimming. Never to sink.

And yet it was exactly what she was doing; sinking into Sakis's eyes, into the miasma of erotic sensations that had reduced her control to nothing. Sensation that had grown with each look, each careless touch, and was now threatening to choke all common sense out of her.

Her hand settled over her heart as if she could

stem its chaotic beating. Then she slowly traced it down, past the scar on her hip to the top of her panties and the heat pooling just below.

The urge to touch herself was strong, almost supernatural. The urge to have stronger, more powerful hands touch her *there* was even more visceral.

Gritting her teeth, she traced her fingers back up to the scar.

Slowly, strength and purpose returned.

Between the tattoo and the scar, she had vivid reminders of why she could never let her guard down again, never trust another human being again. She intended to cling to them with everything she had. Because the purpose she'd seen in Sakis's eyes had scared her.

A determined Sakis was a formidable Sakis.

She would need all the strength she could muster. Because she had a feeling this crisis was far from over; that Sakis would demand more from her than he ever had.

She whirled from the sink and entered the shower. By the time she'd washed the grime off her body, a semblance of calm had returned.

She dried herself and dressed quickly in a T-shirt and the short leggings she used for the gym that—thank God—she'd had the forethought to pack. If she'd been alone, the T-shirt would've sufficed but there was no way she was going out there, sharing a room with Sakis Pantelides, with a thigh-skimming T-shirt and bare legs.

The fiery sensation she'd managed to bank threatened to rise again. Quickly, she brushed her teeth, pulled her hair into its no-nonsense bun and left the bathroom.

Sakis stood outside on the tiny balcony that served the room, a drink in his hand, staring out into the sultry, humid night. His other hand was braced on the iron railing.

She paused and stared as he turned his head. His commanding profile caught and held her attention. His full lower lip was now drawn in a tight line as he stared into the contents of his glass. A wave of bleakness passed over his face and she wondered if he was replaying the journalist's question about his father.

Sakis didn't often display emotion, but she'd seen the way he'd reacted to that personal question. And his answer had been a revelation in itself. He bore no loving memories of his father but he certainly bore scars from his father's legacy.

Unbidden, the earlier wave of protectiveness resurged.

He lifted his glass and swallowed half its contents. Mesmerised, she watched his throat as he swallowed, then her gaze moved to his well-defined chest as he heaved in a huge breath.

*Move!* But she couldn't heed the silent command pounding in her brain. Her feet refused to move. She was still immobilised when he swung towards the room.

He stilled, dark-green eyes zeroing in on her in that fiercely focused, extremely unnerving way.

After several seconds, his gaze travelled over her, head to bare toes, and back again. Slowly, without taking his gaze off her, he downed the rest of his drink. His tongue glided out to lick a drop from his lower lip.

The inferno stormed through her, ravaging her senses with merciless force.

No. Hell, no! This could *not* be happening.

Her fingers tightened around her bag until pain shot up her arms. With brutal force, she wrenched her gaze away, walked towards the sofa and dropped her bag beside it.

'I'm done with the bathroom. It's all yours.' She cringed at the quiver in her voice, a telling barometer of her inner turmoil. Her tablet lay where she'd left it on the table. Itching for something to do with her dangerously restless hands, she grabbed it.

He came towards her and passed within touching distance to set his glass down on the cabinet.

Brianna decided breathing could wait until he was out of scenting range.

'Thanks.' He grabbed his bag and walked to the door. 'And Moneypenny?'

The need to breathe became dangerously imperative but not yet; a few more seconds, until she didn't have to breathe the same air as him. 'Yes?' she managed.

'It's time to clock off.'

The tightness in her chest grew. 'I just wanted to—'

'Turn that tablet off and put it away. That's an order.'

It was either argue with him, or breathe. The need for oxygen won out. She placed the tablet back on the table and stuffed her hands under her thighs.

Satisfaction gleamed in his eyes as he opened the bathroom door. 'Good.' His gaze darted to the bed. 'You take the bed, I'll take the sofa,' he said. Then he entered the bathroom and shut the door behind him.

Brianna sucked in a long, sustaining breath, trying desperately to ignore the traces of Sakis's scent that lingered in the air. She eyed the bed, then the sofa.

The logic was irrefutable. She pulled out and

made up the sofa bed in record time. And she made damned sure she was in it and turned away from the bathroom door by the time she heard the shower go off.

The consequences of giving lust any room was much too great to contemplate. Because giving in to her emotions, trusting it would turn to more—perhaps even the love she'd been blindingly desperate for—was what had landed her in prison.

Being in prison had nearly killed her.

Brianna had no intention of failing. No intention of sinking again.

# CHAPTER FOUR

SHE WOKE TO the smell of strong coffee and an empty room. Relief punched through her as she tossed the light sheet aside and rose from the sofa bed. A quick glance at the ruffled bed showed evidence of Sakis's presence but, apart from that, every last trace of him had been wiped from the room, including his bag.

Before she could investigate further, her tablet pinged with an incoming message.

Grasping it, she tried to get into the zone—business as usual. Just the way she wanted her life to run. Turning the tablet on, she went through the messages as she poured her coffee.

Two of them were from Sakis, who'd taken up residence in the conference room downstairs. Several of them were from people interested in joining the salvage process or blogging about it. But there was still no word about the missing crew.

After answering Sakis's message to join him downstairs as soon as she was ready, she tackled the most important emails, took a quick shower and dressed in a clean pair of khaki combat trousers and a cream T-shirt.

By the time she'd tied her hair into its usual French knot, the events of last night had been consigned a 'temporary aberration' status. Thankfully, she'd been asleep by the time he emerged from the bathroom and, even though she'd woken once and heard his light, even breathing, she'd managed to go back to sleep with no trouble.

Which meant she really didn't have to fear that the rhythm of their relationship had changed.

It hadn't. After this crisis was over, they would return to London and everything would go back to machine-smooth efficiency.

She shrugged on her dark-green jacket, grabbed her case and went downstairs to find Sakis on the phone in the conference room.

He indicated the extensive breakfast tray; she'd just bitten into a piece of honeyed toast when he hung up.

'The salvage crew have contained the leak in the last compartment and the transport tanker for the undamaged oil will arrive in the next few hours.'

'So the damaged tanker can be moved in the next few days?'

He nodded. 'After the International Maritime Investigation Board has completed its investigation it will be tugged back to the ship-building facility in Piraeus. And, now we have a full salvage team in place, there's no need for any remaining crew to stay. They can go home.'

Brianna nodded and brushed crumbs off her fingers. 'I'll arrange it.'

Even though she powered up her tablet ready to action his request, she felt the heat of his gaze on her face.

'You do my bidding without question when it comes to matters of the boardroom. And yet you blatantly disobeyed me last night,' he said in a low voice.

She paused mid-swallow and looked up. Arresting green eyes caught and locked onto hers. 'I'm sorry?'

He twirled a pen in his hand. 'I asked you to take the bed last night. You didn't.'

She forced herself to swallow and tried to look away. She really tried. But it seemed as if he'd charged the very air with a magnetic field that held her captive. 'I didn't think your jump-when-I-say edict extended beyond the boardroom to the bedroom, Mr Pantelides.'

Too late, she realised the indelicacy of her words.

His eyes gleamed with lazy green fire. But she wasn't fooled for a second that it was harmless.

'It doesn't. When it comes to the bedroom, I like control, but I'm not averse to relinquishing it…on occasion.'

Noting that she was in serious danger of going up in flames at the torrid images that cascaded through her mind, she tried to move on. 'Logic dictated that since I'm smaller in stature the sofa would be more suited to me. I didn't see the need for chivalry to get in the way of a good night's sleep for either of us.'

One brow shot up. 'Chivalry? You think I did it out of *chivalry*?' His amusement was unmistakeable.

A damning tide of heat swept up her face. But she couldn't look away from those mesmerising eyes. 'Well, I'm sure you had your own reasons… But I thought…' She huffed. 'It doesn't really matter now, does it?'

'I suggested it because it wouldn't have been a hardship for me.'

'I'm sure it wouldn't, but you don't have a monopoly on pain and discomfort, Mr Pantelides.'

He stiffened. 'Excuse me?'

'I just meant…whatever the circumstances of your past, at least you had a mother who loved you, so it couldn't have been all bad.' She couldn't stem the vein of bitterness from bleeding into her voice, nor could she fail to realise she'd strayed dangerously far from an innocuous subject. But short of blurting out her own past this was the only way she could stop the slippery slope towards believing Sakis cared about her wellbeing.

She'd suffered a childhood hopelessly devoid of love and comfort, and the threat of a life of drugs had been an ever-present reality. Sleeping on a sofa bed was heaven in comparison.

His narrowed eyes speared into her. 'Don't mistake guilt for love, Moneypenny. I've learned over the years that this so-called love is a convenient blanket that's thrown over most feelings.'

She sucked in a breath. 'You don't think that your mother loves you?'

His jaw tightened. 'A weak love is worse than no love. When it crumbles under the weight of adversity it might as well not be present.'

Brianna's fingers tightened around her tablet as shock roiled through her. For the second time in two days, she was glimpsing a whole new facet of Sakis Pantelides.

This was a man who had hidden, painful depths that she'd barely glimpsed in all the time she'd worked for him.

'What adversity?'

He shrugged. 'My mother believed the man she *loved* could do no wrong. When the reality hit her, she chose to give up and leave her children to fend for themselves.' Casually, he flipped his pen in his hand. 'I've been taking care of myself for a very long time, Moneypenny.'

She believed him. She'd always known he possessed a hardened core of steel beneath that urbane façade, but now she knew how it'd been honed, she felt that wave of sympathy and connection again.

Ruthlessly, she tried to reel back the unravelling happening inside her.

'Thanks for sharing that with me. But the sofa was really no hardship for me either and, as long as we're both rested, that should be the end of the subject, surely?'

His eyes remained inscrutable. 'Indeed. I know when to pick my battles, Moneypenny, and I will let this one go.'

The notion that there would be other heated battles between them disturbed her in an altogether too excited way. Before she could respond, he carried on.

'You'll also be happy to know there won't be any need for me to crowd your personal space any longer. Another room has become available. I've taken it.'

Expecting strong relief, she floundered when all she felt was a hard bite of disappointment.

'Great. That's good to know.'

Her tablet pinged a message. Grateful beyond words, she jumped on it.

After breakfast they returned to the site, suited up, and joined the clean-up process. Towards mid-afternoon, she was working alongside Sakis when she felt him tense.

The pithy Greek curse he uttered didn't need translating. 'What the hell are they doing here?'

Her heart sank when she saw the TV crew. 'This is one wave we're just going to have to ride. Nothing I can do to send them away, but I may be able to get them to play nice. You just have to trust me.' The moment the words left her lips, she froze.

So did he. Trust was an issue they both had problems with. She had no business asking for his when she hid a past that could end their relationship in a heartbeat.

But slowly, the look in his eyes changed from hard-edged displeasure to appreciative gleaming. '*Efkharisto*. I have no idea what I'd do without you, Moneypenny,' he said in a low, rumbling voice.

Her heart lurched, then hammered with a force that made her fear for the integrity of her internal organs. 'That's good, because I've devised this cunning plan to make sure that you don't have to.'

A corner of his mouth rose and fell in a swift smile. His gaze dropped to her lips, then rose to recapture hers. 'When Ari threatened to poach you, I nearly knocked him out with my oar,' he said, his voice rumbling in that gravel-rough pitch that made the muscles in her stomach flutter and tighten.

'I wouldn't have gone.' Not in a million years. She loved working with Sakis, even if the last two days had sent her on a knuckle-rattling emotional rollercoaster.

'Good. You belong to me and I have no intention of letting you go. I'll personally annihilate anyone who tries to take you away from me.'

Her pulse raced faster. *Work. He's talking about your professional relationship. Not making a statement of personal intent.* Brianna forced that reminder on her erratic senses and tried to breathe normally. When her belly continued to roil, she sucked in air through her mouth.

Sakis made a small, hoarse sound in his throat. Heat arched between them, making her skin tingle and the flesh between her legs ache with desperate need.

Hastily she took a step back. 'I…I'll go and speak to the TV crew.'

She turned and fled. And with every step she prayed desperately for her equilibrium to return.

The TV crew refused to leave but agreed not to interview any member of the crew. For that she had to be content.

Sakis's meeting with the maritime disaster investigators went smoothly because he had already admitted liability and agreed to make reparations, and he barely blinked at the mind-bogglingly heavy fine they imposed on Pantelides Inc.

But his behaviour with her was anything but smooth. Throughout the meeting, Sakis would turn to her for her opinion, touch her arm to draw her attention to something he needed written down or shoot her a question. Fear coursed through her as she realised that the almost staid, rigidly professional team they'd been seventy-two hours ago had all but disappeared.

By the time the meeting concluded, she knew she was in trouble.

Sakis pushed a frustrated hand through his hair and paced the conference room, anger beating beneath his skin. The investigators had just confirmed the accident was human error.

Striding to his desk, he threw himself in the chair.

'Has Morgan Lowell's file arrived yet?' he asked Brianna.

She came towards him and he tried not to let his gaze drop to the sway of her hips. All damned day, he'd found himself checking her out. He'd even stopped asking himself what the hell was wrong with him because he knew.

Lust.

Untrammelled, bloody, lust. From the easily controlled attraction he'd felt when he'd first met her, it now threatened to drown him with every single breath he took in her presence.

She held out the information he'd asked for and he tried not to stare at the delicate bones of her wrist.

'What do we know about him?' he asked briskly.

'He's married; no children; his wife lives with his parents. As far as we can tell, he's the sole provider for his family. And he's been with the company the last four years. He came straight from the navy, where he was a commander.'

'I know all of that.' He flicked past the personal details to the work history and paused, a tingle of unease whispering down his spine. 'It says here he's refused to take leave in the last three years. And he's been married…just over three years. Why would a newly wedded man not want to be with his wife?'

'Perhaps he had something to prove, or something to hide,' came the stark, terse response.

Surprised, he glanced up. Unease slid through her blue eyes before she lowered them. He continued to stare, and right before his eyes his normally serenely professional PA became increasingly… flustered. The intrigue that had dogged him since seeing that damned tattoo on her ankle rose even higher.

He sat back in his chair. 'Interesting observation, Moneypenny. What makes you say that?'

She bit her lip and blood roared through his veins. 'I…didn't mean anything by it. Certainly nothing based on solid fact.'

'But you said it anyway. Instinctive or not, you suspect there's something else going on here, no?'

She shrugged. 'It was just a general comment, gleaned from observing natural human behaviour. Most people fall into one of those two categories. It could be that Captain Lowell falls into both.' She firmed her lips as if she wanted to prevent any more words from spilling out.

'What do you mean?' he asked. Impatience grew when she just shook her head. 'Come on, you have a theory. Let's hear it.'

'I just think the fact that both Lowell and his two deputies are missing is highly questionable. I can't think why all three would be away from the bridge and not respond when the alarm was raised.'

Ice slammed into his chest. 'The investigators think it was human error but you think it was deliberate?' Reactivating the tablet, he flicked through the rest of Morgan Lowell's work history but nothing in there threw up any red flags.

On paper, his missing captain was an extremely competent leader with solid credentials who'd piloted the Pantelides tanker efficiently for the last four years.

*On paper.*

Sakis knew first-hand that 'on paper' meant nothing when it came right down to it.

*On paper* Alexandrou Pantelides, his father, had been an honourable, hard-working and generous father to those who hadn't known better. Only Sakis, his brothers and mother had known it was a façade he presented to the world. It was only when a scorned lover had tipped off a hungry journalist who'd chosen to dig a little deeper that the truth had emerged. A truth that had unearthed a rotten trough full of discarded mistresses and shady business dealings that had overnight heaped humiliation and devastation on the innocent.

*On paper* Giselle had seemed an efficient, healthily ambitious executive assistant, until Sakis's rejection of her one late-night advance had unearthed a spiteful, cold-blooded, psychopathic nature that had threatened to destabilise his company's very foundation.

'On paper' meant nothing if he couldn't look into Lowell's eyes, ask what had happened and get a satisfactory answer.

'We need to find him, Moneypenny,' he bit out, bitterness replacing the ice in his chest. 'There's too much at stake here to leave this unresolved for much longer.' For one thing, the media would spin itself out of control if word of this got out. 'Contact the head of security. Tell them to dig deeper into Lowell's background.'

Sakis looked up in time to see Brianna pale a little. 'Is something wrong?' he asked.

Her mouth showed the tiniest hint of a twist. 'No.'

His gaze dropped to hands that would normally be flying over her tablet as she rushed to do his bidding. They were clasped together, unmoving. 'Something obviously is.'

Darkened eyes met his and he saw rebellion lurking in their depths. 'I don't think it's fair to dig into someone's life just because you have a hunch.'

Her words held brevity that made Sakis frown. 'Did you not suggest minutes ago that Lowell could be hiding something?'

She gave a reluctant nod.

'Then shouldn't we try and find out what that something *is*?'

'I suppose.'

'But?'

'I think he deserves for his life not to be turned inside out on a hunch. And I'm sorry if I gave you the impression that was what I wanted, because it's not.'

A tic throbbed in his temple. Restlessness made him shove away from the desk. His stride carried him to the window and back to the desk next to where she sat, unmoving fingers resting on her tablet.

'Sometimes we have to bear the consequences of unwanted scrutiny for the greater good.' As much as he'd detested the hideous fallout, having his father's true colours exposed had ultimately been to his benefit. He'd learned to look beneath the surface. Always.

She looked at him. 'You're advocating something

that you hated having done to you. How did you feel when your family's secrets were exposed to the whole world?'

Shock slammed into him at her sheer audacity. Planting his hands on the desk, he lowered his head until his gaze was level with hers. '*Excuse me?* What the hell do you think you know about my family?' he rasped.

She drew back a touch but her gaze remained unflinching. 'I know what happened with your father when you were a teenager. The Internet makes information impossible to hide. And your reaction to the tabloid hack's question yesterday—'

'There was *no* reaction.'

'I was there. I saw how much you hated it.' Her voice was soft with sympathy.

The idea of being pitied made his fist tighten on the table.

'And you think this should make me bury my head in the sand about Lowell?'

'No, I'm just saying that turning his life inside out doesn't feel right. Since you've been in his shoes—'

'Since I don't know anything more than what his human resources file says, that's a lofty conclusion to draw. And, unlike what you think you know about me and my family, what I find out about Captain Lowell won't find its way to the tabloid press or any social media forum for the world at large to feast over and make caricatures out of. So I say no, there is *nothing* even remotely similar between the two situations.'

She drew in a slow, steady breath. 'If you say so.' Her gaze dropped and she pulled the tablet towards her.

Sakis stayed exactly where he was, the urge to invade her space further an almighty need that stomped through him. In the last twenty-four hours, his PA had acted out of character, challenged him in ways she'd never done before.

The incident with the tent and the sleeping on the sofa bed, he was willing to let go. This latest challenge—breaching the taboo subject of his father—should've made him fire her on the spot. But, as much as he hated to admit it, she was right. The journalist's question *had* shaken him and unearthed volcanic feelings he preferred masked.

In silence, he watched her compose a succinct email to his security chief, stating his exact wishes.

The electronic 'whoosh' of the outgoing email perforated the silence in the conference room. It was as if the very air was holding its breath.

Brianna raised her head after setting the tablet down. 'Is there anything else?'

His gaze traced over her. A tendril of hair had escaped its tight prison and caressed the wild pulse beating in her neck. His fingers tingled with the need to smooth it away and trace the pulse with his fingers; to keep tracing down the length of her sleek neck to the delicate collarbone hidden beneath her T-shirt.

'You disagree with what I'm doing?'

Her full pink lips firmed. That dimple winked again. His groin tightened unbearably.

'Privacy is a right and I detest those who breach it. I know you do too, so I'm struggling with this a little, but I also get why it needs to be done. I also apologise if I stepped out of line but...I trust you when you say you won't let it fall into unscrupulous hands.'

Her last words drilled down and touched a soft place inside him, soothed the ruffled edge of his nerves a little. 'You have my word that whatever we discover about Lowell will be held in strictest confidence.' The knowledge that he was reassuring her, was justifying his behaviour to his assistant, threw him a little, as did the knowledge that he *wanted* her to approve of what he was doing. He pushed the feeling away as she nodded.

The movement slid the silky hair against her nape. The soft scent of her crushed-lilies shampoo hit his nostrils and his fingers renewed their mad tingling.

'And, Moneypenny?'

She glanced up. This close, her eyes were even more enthralling. His heart raced and his blood rushed south with a need so forceful, he sucked in a shocked breath.

'Yes?' Her lips were parted, the tip of her wet tongue peeking through even teeth.

Sakis struggled to remember what he'd meant to say. 'I don't trust easily but that doesn't mean I don't appreciate people who place their trust in me. In all the time you've worked for me, you've proved yourself trustworthy and someone I can rely on. Your help especially in the past two days has been priceless. Thank you.'

Her eyed widened. God, she was beautiful. How the hell had he never noticed that?

'Of...of course, Mr Pantelides.'

Curiously, she paled a little bit more. Sakis frowned then chalked it down to exhaustion. They'd both been driven by dire circumstances to the pinnacle of their endurance. He needed to let her go to her room instead of crouching over her like some dark lord about to demand a virgin sacrifice.

He grimaced and stepped back, slamming down

the need to stay where he was. Tension stretched over every of inch of his skin until he felt taut and uncommonly sensitive. 'I think we find ourselves in a unique enough situation where it's okay for you to call me Sakis.'

She shook her head. 'No.'

His brow shot up. 'Just…*no*?'

'I'm sorry, but I can't.' Edging away from him, she sprang to her feet. 'If that's all you need tonight, I'll say goodnight.'

'Goodnight…Brianna.' Her name sounded like the sweetest temptation on his lips.

She hesitated. 'I would really prefer it if you kept calling me Moneypenny,' she said.

Immediate refusal rose to his lips. Until he remembered he was supposed to be her unimpeachable boss, not a demanding lover who was at this moment repeating her given name over and over in his mind. 'Very well. See you in the morning, Moneypenny.'

He straightened from the table and watched her walk away, her pert bottom tight and deliciously curvy beneath her khaki pants, causing blood to rush hot and fast southward.

He still sported a hard-on that wouldn't die when his phone rang in his suite an hour later. He stopped pacing his small balcony long enough to snag it from the coffee table where he'd dumped it.

'Pantelides.'

The short conversation that ensued made him curse long and fluently for several minutes after he hung up.

# CHAPTER FIVE

THE FIRM HAMMERING on her door made Brianna's already racing heart threaten to knock itself into early retirement. Considering the way it'd been racing for the past hour—ever since her wits had deserted her in the conference room—it would've been merciful.

What the hell had she been *thinking*?

Hard knuckles gave the wooden door another impatient workout.

Consciously loosening her tense shoulders, she blew out a reassuring breath and forced composure back into her body. The hastily pulled together bland look was in place when she answered the door.

Sakis stood on the threshold, frowning down at his phone.

'What's wrong?' she asked before she could stop herself. The feeling that passed through her, she recognised as worry, a curiously recurring feeling over the past two days. *Not cool, Brianna.* In fact, a wincingly large percentage of her reactions today had been…off. From the moment he'd stared down at her and told her in that mesmerising voice, 'I don't know what I'd do without you,' her judgement had been skewed.

Watching him pace with mounting frustration all day, wishing there was something she could do, had rammed home the fact that her professional equanimity was still very much in jeopardy.

Now…now he looked as if he'd clawed frustrated fingers through his hair several times. And the lines bracketing his mouth had deepened. She cleared her throat.

'I mean, is there something you need, Mr Pantelides?'

His gaze flicked over her then returned to her face. 'You haven't changed for bed yet. Good. The pilot is readying the chopper for take-off in fifteen minutes.'

'Take-off?'

His hand tightened around the phone as it signalled another incoming message. 'We're leaving for the airport. I've called an emergency meeting first thing in the morning back in London.'

'We're returning to London? But…why?'

His lips firmed. 'It seems more vultures are circling over our disaster.'

Stunned, she stared at him. The thought that anyone would want to challenge Sakis Pantelides at any time, let alone when he was at his most edgy and dangerous, made her doubt his opponent's sanity. 'Media or corporate?'

His smile was deadly. 'Corporate. I'm guessing the usual suspects who chest-thump every now and then will be feeling bolder in light of the slumping share price as a result of the tanker accident.'

She retrieved the bag she'd left at the foot of her bed. 'But the shares have started to recover again after the initial nosedive. Your statement and the very public admission of liability made it stabilise very quickly. Why would they…?'

'News of a takeover bid would make it plunge again and that's what they're counting on.' His phone pinged again and he growled. 'Especially if two of those companies are announcing their intended merger in the morning.'

He cursed in Greek, using a particular word that made heat rise to her cheeks as she dove into the bathroom for her toiletries bag.

'Which two companies?' she called out as she zipped up her bag and checked the room to make sure she hadn't left anything important.

Exiting, she saw the lines of fatigue etched into his face and her heart lurched.

'Moorecroft Oil and Landers Petroleum.'

It was only because he'd turned away, his attention once more on this phone, that Sakis didn't see she'd stopped dead in her tracks; that the blood had drained from her face with a swiftness that made her dizzy for a moment.

*It couldn't be.* No. It had to be pure coincidence that the petroleum company shared the same name with Greg, her ex-boyfriend. Landers was a fairly common name…wasn't it? Besides, Greg's company when she'd been a part of it before he'd struck the deal that had doomed her, had been a gas-brokering company; a company that had since declared bankruptcy. And certainly not one large enough to take on the juggernaut that was Pantelides Shipping.

'I'd like to get out of here this side of— Brianna? What's wrong?'

*For goodness' sake, pull yourself together!*

Dry-mouthed and heart thumping, Brianna forced herself to breathe. 'Nothing; it's the heat, I think.'

Keen eyes scoured her face and gentled a fraction as he pocketed his phone. 'Not to mention the lack of sleep. My apologies for dragging you off like this. You can sleep on the plane.'

Stepping forward, he held out his hand for her

bag. Their fingers touched, lingered. Heat shot through her and she hastily pulled back from the scorching contact. Swallowing, she followed him out and shut the door behind her. 'I'll be fine. And you'll need me to find out everything we can about the two companies.' Not to mention *she* needed to know whether Greg had anything to do with Landers Petroleum.

The thought that he might have started another company, might be cultivating another patsy the same way he'd cultivated her, made her stomach lurch sickeningly.

Could she alert Sakis without drawing attention to herself? Out herself as the needy woman, so desperate for love she hadn't seen the trap set for her until it'd been too late?

Her belly churned with fear and anxiety as they left the hotel and rode the short helicopter journey to the private hangar at Agostinho Neto airport.

*Dear God. She could lose everything.*

The thought sent a shudder so strong, she stumbled over her own feet a few steps from the airplane.

Sakis caught her arm and steadied her. Then his fingers dropped to encircle her wrist, keeping a firm hold on her as he mounted the steps into the plane.

She swallowed down the wholly different trepidation that stemmed from having Sakis's hand on her. She tried to pull away, but he held on until they stood before the guest-cabin bedroom opposite the plane's master suite. He opened the door and set her bag down just inside it, then led her back to the seating area.

At Sakis's signal, the pilot shut the door.

'Buckle up. Right after we take off, we're going to bed.'

Her mouth dropped open as her pulse shot sky-high. '*I beg your pardon*?' she squeaked. Her whole body throbbed and she couldn't glance away from his disturbingly direct gaze.

His grim smile held a wealth of masculine arrogance as he shoved a frustrated hand through his hair. Taking his seat opposite her, he set his phone—which had thankfully stopped pinging—on a nearby table. 'A…poor choice of words, Moneypenny. What I mean is, it's the middle of the night in London. Not much we can do from here.'

'I can still pull up as much information as I can on the companies…'

He shook his head. 'I already have people working on that. You need to get some sleep. I need you sharp and—'

'You need to stop treating me like some fragile flower and let me do my job!'

Moss-green eyes narrowed. 'Excuse me?'

Anger lent her voice desperation and she leaned forward, hands planted on the table separating them. The fact that this close she could almost touch the stubble layering his hard, chiselled jaw and see the darker, mesmerising flecks in his irises sparked another tingle of awareness through her. But the remotest possibility that Greg could be lurking in the periphery of her life, ready to expose her, made her stand her ground.

She'd gone through too much, sacrificing everything she had to prevent her debilitating weakness from being exposed. She no longer needed love. She'd learned that she could live without it. What she couldn't live with was having her previous sins exposed to Sakis Pantelides.

'You seem to think I need a full night's sleep or a warm bed to function properly, but that couldn't be farther from the truth.' Warning bells rang in her head, telling her seriously to apply brakes on her runaway mouth. But she couldn't help herself. 'I've slept in places where I had to keep one eye open or risk losing more than just the clothes on my back. So please don't treat me like some pampered princess who needs her beauty sleep or she'll go to pieces.'

His eyes narrowed, followed almost instantly by a keen speculation that screamed what was coming next. 'When did you sleep rough?' His voice was low, husky, full of unabashed curiosity.

Alarm bells shrieked harder, in tandem with the jet engines powering for take-off. Sharp memories rose, images of drug dens and foul-smelling narcotics bringing nausea she fought to keep down. 'It doesn't matter.'

He leaned forward on his elbows and stared her down. 'Yes, it does. Answer me.'

'It was a very long time ago, Mr Pantelides.'

'Sakis,' he commanded in that low, deep tone that sent a shiver through her.

Again she shook her head. 'Let's just say my childhood wasn't as rosy as the average child's, but I pulled through.'

'You were an orphan?' he probed.

'No, I wasn't, but I might as well have been.' Because her junkie mother had been no use to herself, never mind the child she'd given birth to. The remembered pain bruised her insides and unshed tears burned the backs of her eyes. She blinked rapidly to stop them falling but a furtive glance showed Sakis had noticed the crack in her composure.

The plane lifted off the ground and shot into the starlit sky.

Sakis's gaze remained on her for long minutes. 'Do you want to talk about it?' he asked gently.

Brianna's heart hammered harder. 'No.' She'd already said too much, revealed far more than was wise. Deliberately unclenching her fists, she prayed he would let the matter rest.

The jet started to level out. Snatching his phone from the table, Sakis nodded and unbuckled his seatbelt. 'Regardless of your protests, you need to sleep.' He held out his hand to her. The look on his face told her nothing but her acquiescence would please him.

Immensely relieved that he wasn't probing into her past any longer, she thought it wise to stifle further protest. Unbuckling her seatbelt, she placed her hand in his and stood. 'If I do, then so do you.'

His smile was unexpected. And breath-stealing. Heat churned within her belly, sending an arrow of need straight between her thighs.

'We've dovetailed right back to the very point I was trying to make. I have every intention of getting some sleep. Even super-humans like me deserve some down time.'

A smile tugged at her lips. 'That's a relief. You were beginning to show us mere mortals up.'

His smile turned into an outright laugh, his face transforming into such a spectacular vision of gorgeousness that her breath caught. Then her whole body threatened to spontaneously combust when his hand settled at her waist. With a firm nudge, he guided her back down the aisle.

'No one in their right mind would call you a mere mortal, Moneypenny. You've proved beyond any doubt that you're the real thing—an exceptionally gifted individual with a core of integrity that most ambitious people lose by the time they reach your age.'

At the door to her cabin, she turned to face him, her heart hammering hard enough to make her head hurt a little. 'I think what you've done since the tanker crashed shows you're willing to go above and beyond what most people would do in the same circumstances. *That* is integrity.'

His gaze dropped to her lips, lingered there in a way that turned her body furnace hot. 'Hmm, is this the start of an exclusive mutual admiration society?'

The breath she'd never quite managed to recapture fractured even further. When his eyes dropped lower, her nipples tightened, stung into life by green fire that lurked in those depths. Reaching behind her, she grasped the doorknob, desperate for something to cling to.

'I'm just trying to point out that I'm nothing special, Mr Pantelides. I just try to be very good at my job.'

His gaze recaptured hers. 'I beg to differ. I think you're very special.' He stepped closer and his scent filled her nostrils. 'It's also obvious no one has told you that enough.' The hand that still rested at her waist slid away to cover the hand she'd gripped on the door. Using the pressure of hers, he turned the knob. 'When this is all over, I'll make a point to show you just how special you are.'

The door gave way behind her and she swayed backward, barely managing to catch herself before she stumbled. 'You...don't have to. Really, you don't.'

His smile was a touch strained and he braced his hands on the doorjamb as if forcibly stopping himself from entering the room. 'You say you're not special and yet you refuse even the promise of a reward where most people would be making a list.'

'I work for one of the most forward-thinking men in one of the best organisations in the world. That's reward enough.'

'Careful, there; you're in danger of swelling my ego to unthinkable proportions.'

'Is that a bad thing?' She wasn't sure where the need for banter came from but her breath caught when his sensual lips curved in a dangerously sexy smile.

'At a time when everything around me seems to be falling apart, it could be a lethal thing.' His gaze shot to the bed and his smile slipped a fraction, in proportion to the escalating strain on his face. 'Time for you to hit the sack. *Kalispera*, Brianna,' he murmured softly before, stepping back abruptly, he strode to his own door.

At the click of his door shutting, Brianna stumbled forward and sagged onto the bed, her knees turned to water.

She glanced down at her shaking hands as reality hit her square in the face.

Sakis Pantelides found her attractive. She wasn't naïve enough to mistake the look in his eyes, nor was she going to waste time contemplating the *why*. It was there, like a ticking time bomb between them, one she needed to diffuse before the unthinkable happened.

Brianna could only hope that, once they were back on familiar ground, things would return to normal.

*They had to.* Because, frankly, she was terrified of what she would let happen if they didn't.

Sakis stood under the cold shower and cursed fluidly. *Theos.* I seemed as if he'd spent the last forty-eight hours cursing in one form or the other. Right now, he cursed the rigid erection that seemed determined to defy the frigid temperature.

He wanted to have sex with Brianna Moneypenny. Wanted to shut off the shower, stride next door, strip the clothes off her body and drive into her with a grinding force that defied rhyme or reason.

He slapped his palm against the soaked tile and cursed some more. Gritting his teeth, his hand dropped to grip his erection. A single stroke made him groan out loud. Another stroke, and his knees threatened to buckle.

With an angry grunt, he dropped his hand and turned the shower off. He was damned if he was going to fondle himself like an over-eager teenager. Things were fraught for sure. That and the fact that he hadn't had sex in months was messing with his mental faculties, making him contemplate paths he would never otherwise have done. For God's sake, sex had no place in his immediate to-do list.

What he needed to do was focus on getting the

threat of a takeover annihilated and the situation at Pointe Noire brought under control.

Once they were back on familiar ground, things would return to normal.

He ruthlessly silenced the voice that mocked him not to be so sure…

Three hours later, Brianna sat wide awake in her luxurious cabin bed, staring through a porthole at the pitch-black night that rested on a bed of white clouds. She'd left her tablet in one of the two briefcases she'd seen the stewardess stow in Sakis's cabin. Short of knocking on his door and asking for it, she had nothing to do but sit here, her thoughts jumbling into a mass of anxiety at what awaited her in London.

She had no doubt Sakis would trounce the takeover bid into smithereens—he was too skilled a businessman not to have anticipated such a move. And he was too calculating not to have the answers at his fingertips.

All the same, Greg had proved, much to her shock and disbelief, that he was just as ruthless—and without a single ounce of integrity—and she shuddered at the chaos he could bring to Sakis should he be given the opportunity.

Her shoulder tingled as her tattoo burned. Raising her hand, she slid her fingers under her light T-shirt and touched the slightly raised words etched into her skin.

Greg had succeeded in taking away her livelihood once; had come terrifyingly close to destroying her soul.

There was no way she could rest until she made sure he wasn't a threat to Sakis and to her. Not that he had any reason to seek her out. No, she was the gullible scapegoat he'd led to the slaughter—then walked away from scot-free. The last thing he'd expect was for her to have risen from the ashes of the fire he'd thrown her in.

That was how she wanted things to stay. Once upon a time, she'd harboured feelings of revenge and retribution; how could she not, when she'd been stuck in an six-by-eight dark space, racked alternatively with fear and deep bitterness? But those feelings had burned themselves out.

Now she just wanted to be Brianna Moneypenny, executive assistant to Sakis Pantelides, the most dynamically sexy, astoundingly intelligent man she knew.

A man she'd come disastrously close to kissing more than once in the last forty-eight hours...

No. Her fingers pressed down harder over the

tattoo, letting the pain of each word restore her equilibrium.

Nothing had changed.

Nothing *could* change.

The board members were gathered in the large, grey mosaic-tiled conference room on the fiftieth floor of Pantelides Towers, the iconic, futuristically designed building poised on the edge of the River Thames.

Sakis strode in at seven o'clock sharp. He nodded to the men around the table and the three executives video-conferencing in on three wide screens.

Brianna's heart thumped as she followed him in. She had no idea if the information-gathering Sakis had implemented before they'd boarded the plane had yielded any results. He didn't know either—she'd asked him. Only the files currently placed in front of each executive held the answer as to whether Greg Landers was in part behind this hostile takeover bid.

Seeing a spare copy on the stationery table off to one side of the boardroom, Brianna moved towards it.

'I won't need you for this meeting. Return to the office. I'll come and find you when I'm done.'

Shock ricocheted through her. She barely managed to keep it from showing on her face. 'Are you sure? I can—'

His jaw tensed. 'I think we've already established that you're invaluable to me. Please don't overplay your hand, Moneypenny. Otherwise alarm bells will start ringing.'

The tight grit behind his words took her aback. It was the same tone he'd used since he'd emerged from his cabin an hour before they'd landed. His whole façade was icily aloof and the potent sexual charge that had surrounded them a few short hours before, the fire in his eyes as he'd looked at her outside her cabin on the plane, was nowhere in sight.

She held her breath for the relief that confirmed that things were back to normal, only to experience a painful pang of disconcerting disappointment, immediately followed by a more terrifying notion.

Did Sakis know? Had he somehow found out about her past? She stared at him but his expression gave nothing away, certainly nothing that indicated he knew her deepest, darkest secret.

He didn't know. She'd been much too careful in exorcising her past; had used every last penny she'd owned two years ago to ensure there would be no coming back from what she'd been before.

All the same, it took a huge effort to swallow

the lump in her throat. 'I don't… I'm not sure I know what you're talking about. I'm only trying to do—'

'Your job. I know. But right now your job isn't here. I need you to take point on the situation on Point Noire. Make sure the media are kept in line and the investigators update us on developments. I don't want the ball dropped on this. Can you handle that?'

Her gaze slid to the file marked confidential lying so innocuously on the table, fear and trepidation eating away inside her. Then she forced her gaze to meet his. 'Of course.'

The hard glint in his eyes softened a touch. 'Good. I'll see you in a few hours. Or sooner, if anything needs my attention.'

He stepped into the room and the electronic door slid shut behind him. Brianna gasped at the bereft feeling that hollowed out her stomach.

*He isn't shutting you out. It's just a delicate situation that needs careful handling.*

Nevertheless, as she walked back towards her office and desk situated just outside Sakis's massive office suite, she couldn't help but feel like she'd lost a part of her functioning self.

Ridiculous.

For the next several hours, she threw herself

into her work. At two o'clock on the button, her phone rang.

'I haven't had an update in four hours,' came Sakis's terse demand.

'That's because everything's in hand. You have enough on your plate without resorting to micro-management,' she snapped, then bit her lip. She was letting her anxiety get the better of her. 'What I mean is, you have the right people in place to deal with this. Let them do their jobs. It's what you pay them for, after all.'

'Duly noted.' A little bit of the terseness had leached from his voice but the strain still remained. She could barely hold back from asking the question burning on her lips: *is Greg Landers one of those challenging to take over Pantelides Shipping*? 'Update me anyway.'

'The tug boat is on site and preparing to move the tanker away. The salvage crew co-ordinator tells me our marine biologist is providing invaluable advice, so we scored big there.'

'*You* scored big.' His voice had dropped lower, grown more intimate. A fresh tingle washed over her.

'Um…I guess. The social media campaign has garnered almost a million followers and the feedback shows a high percentage support Pantelides

Shipping's stance on the salvage and clean-up process. The blogger is doing a superb job, too.'

'Brianna?'

'Yes?'

'I'm glad I took your advice about the media campaign. It's averted a lot of the bad press we could've had with this crash.'

Her normal, professional, politically correct answer faded on her tongue. Heart hammering, she gripped the phone harder and spoke from the heart. 'I care about this company. I didn't want to see its reputation suffer.'

'Why? Why do you care?' His voice had dropped even lower.

'You…you gave me a chance when I thought I would have none. You could've chosen someone else from over a hundred applicants for this job. You chose me. I don't take that lightly.'

'Don't sell yourself short, Brianna. I didn't pick your name out of a box. I picked you because you're special. And you continue to prove to me every day what a valuable asset you are.'

She loved the way he said her name. The realisation sent a pulse of heat rushing through her.

'Thank you, Mr Pantelides.'

'Sakis,' came the rumbled response.

She shook her head in immediate refusal, even

though he couldn't see her. 'N…no,' she finally managed.

'I *will* get you to call me Sakis before very long.' His voice held a rough texture that made her tremble.

Closing her eyes, she forced herself to breathe and focus. 'How are things going with the…the board meeting?'

'Most of the key players have been identified. I've fired the warning shot. They can heed it or they can choose to come at me again.' His words held a distinct relish that made her think he almost welcomed the challenge of his authority. Sakis was a man who needed an outlet for his passions, hence the rowing when he could, and the fully equipped gyms in his penthouse and homes all around the world.

*He would be just as passionate in the bedroom.* She hurriedly pushed the thought away.

'Have we heard anything else?' he asked, his voice turning brisk once more.

She knew he meant the missing crew. 'No, nothing. The search parameters have been widened.' And because she feared what would spill from her lips if she hung on, she said, 'I need to make a few more phone calls; rearrange your schedule…'

He went silent for several seconds, then he

sighed. 'If Lowell's wife calls, put her straight through to me.'

'I will.' She hung up quickly before she could ask about what he'd found out. Unwilling even to think of it, she threw herself back to her work.

At six, the executive chef Sakis employed for his senior staff poked his head through her office door and asked if she wanted dinner.

She rolled her shoulders, registered the stiffness in her body and shook her head.

'I'm going to hit the gym first, Tom. Then I'll forage for myself, thanks.'

He nodded and left.

Picking up her phone and tablet, she quickly made her way via the turbo lift to the sixtieth floor, where Sakis's private multi-roomed penthouse suites were located. There were six suites in total, four separate and two inter-connected. Sakis used the largest suite which was linked by a set of double doors to her own suite when she stayed here. From this high, the view across London's night sky was stunning. The Opera House gleamed beneath the iconic London Eye, with the Oxo Tower's famous lights glittering over the South Bank.

She took the shortcut through Sakis's living room, her feet slowing as they usually did when confronted with the visually stunning architectural design of the penthouse.

One side was taken up by a rough sandstone wall dominated by a huge fireplace regulated by a computerised temperature monitor. Directly in front of the fireplace, large slate-coloured, square-shaped sofas were grouped around an enormous stark white rug, which was the only covering on the highly polished marble floors.

Beyond the seating area, on carefully selected pedestals and on the walls were displayed works of art ranging from an exquisite pair of katanas, said to have belonged to a notorious Samurai, to a post-impressionist painting by Rousseau that galleries around the world vied for the opportunity to exhibit.

Moving towards her own suite, her gaze was drawn outside to the gleaming infinity pool that stretched out beyond the gleaming windows. The first time she'd seen it, she'd gasped with awe and thanked her lucky stars that she didn't suffer from vertigo when Sakis had shown her around the large deck where the only protection from the elements was a steel and glass railing.

From this high up, the Thames was a dark ribbon interspersed by centuries-old bridges, and from where she stood she could almost make out the Tube station where she caught the train to her flat.

Her flat. Her sanctuary. The place she hadn't been for days. The place she could lose if Sakis ever found out who she really was.

Her spine straightened as she approached the large wooden swivel door that led to her suite.

As long as she had breath in her body she would fight for what she'd salvaged from the embers of her previous life. Greg wouldn't be allowed to win a second time.

Entering the bedroom where Sakis had insisted she kept a fully furnished wardrobe in case he needed to travel with her at short notice, she changed into her pair of three-quarter-length Lycra training shorts and a cropped T-shirt.

She pounded the treadmill for half an hour, until endorphins pumped through her system and sweat poured off her skin. Next she tackled the elliptical trainer.

She was in the middle of stretching before hitting the weights when Sakis walked in.

He stopped at the sight of her. His hair was severely ruffled, the result of running his hands through the short strands several times, and he'd loosened his tie, along with a few buttons. Between the gaping cotton, she saw silky hairs that bisected his deep, chiselled chest.

Their eyes clashed through the mirrors lining two sides of the room, before his gaze left her to slowly traverse over her body.

Brianna froze, very much aware her breath was caught somewhere in her solar plexus. And that her leg was caught behind her, mid-stretch. The hand braced against the mirror trembled as his gaze visibly darkened with a hunger that echoed the sensation spiking up through her pelvis.

'Don't let me interrupt you,' he drawled as he went to the cooler and plucked a bottle of water off the shelf. Leaning against the rung of bars holding the weights, he stared at her as he drank deeply straight from the bottle.

She tried not to let her eyes devour the sensual movement of his throat as he swallowed. With a deep breath that cost her every ounce of self-control she possessed, she lifted and grabbed her other foot behind her, extending her body into a taut stretch, while studiously avoiding his gaze.

She'd never been more aware of the tightness of her gym clothes or the sheen of sweat coating her skin. Thankfully, she'd secured her hair so tight it hadn't escaped its bun...yet.

Sinking low, she extended in a sideways stretch

that made her inner thigh muscles scream. Her heartbeat was hammering so loudly in her ears, she was sure she'd imagined Sakis's sharp indrawn breath.

Silence grew around them until she couldn't bear being the sole focus of his gaze. Rising after her last stretch, she contemplated the wisdom of approaching where he stood, right in front of the weights she needed.

Contemplated and abandoned the idea. Instead, she mimicked him and went to the well-stocked fridge for a bottle of water. 'How did the rest of the board meeting go?' she asked to fill the heavy silence.

Sakis tossed the empty bottle in the recycle bin, pulled his tie free, rolled it up and stuffed it in his trouser pocket. 'I had no doubt we would find the relevant weak points. Everyone has skeletons in their closets, Moneypenny. Things they don't want anyone else to discover. Growing up as a Pantelides taught me that.' His voice was pure steel, but she caught the underlying thread of pain beneath it.

She wanted to offer comforting words but the mention of skeletons sliced her with apprehension, tightening her insides so she could barely breathe. 'What sort of skeletons?'

'The usual. In this case, less than stellar financial record-keeping; one or two shady dealings that deserve closer scrutiny.'

'Are…are we talking about Landers Petroleum?' She held her breath.

'No.' He dismissed them with a wave of his hand. 'They're small fry compared to Moorecroft Oil and were probably hitching their wagon to the big boys in hopes of a large pay-day. For now, I'm more interested in Moorecroft. They're the ones who started this, but they should've cleaned up their own backyard before attempting to sully mine. Tomorrow morning, their CEO, Richard Moorecroft, will be receiving a call from the Financial Conduct Authority. He'll need to answer a few hairy questions.'

She told herself it was too early to hope this was over but she allowed herself a tiny breath of relief. 'And…you think that's the end of it?'

His hand went to the next unopened button and slid it free. 'If they know what's good for them. If they don't and they keep sabre-rattling, things will just get decidedly…dirtier.'

'You mean you'll dig deeper,' she murmured, unable to take her gaze off the hands slowly revealing more and more of his mouth-watering torso. 'What are you doing?' she gasped, her fist tightening around the plastic bottle as another bolt of heat drilled through her belly. It cracked under the force of her fist, echoing loudly through the room.

'Taking a leaf out of your book.' He shrugged out of his shirt, balled it up and threw it into the corner.

'I… But…'

He paused, his hand on his belt. 'Does my body make you uncomfortable, Moneypenny?'

Her tongue threatened to not work. 'You've undressed in front of me many times.'

'That wasn't what I asked you.' The belt slid free.

Arousal roared to life, tightening her nipples into deliciously painful points, weakening her knees, shooting fiery sensation between her legs. 'W…what does it matter? I'm invisible, remember? You've never seen me in the past.'

He came forward, his long legs eating up the short distance between them until he stood in front of her.

'Only because I've trained myself not to look… not to betray the slightest interest. Not since…' He paused, lips pursed. Then, shaking off whatever thought he'd had, he shrugged. 'You're not invisible to me now. I see you. *All* of you.' His gaze slid down, paused and caressed the valley between her breasts, before reaching out to boldly stroke the hard, pointed crests. Her needy gasp made him caress her more intimately, rolling her nipple between his fingers until she had to bite her lip hard to keep from crying out. 'And just like I knew you would be like...a potent wine, promising intoxication even before the first sip.'

Reason tried to surge forth through the miasma of sensation shaking her very foundations. But her body had a mind of its own. It swayed towards him but she managed to stop herself from taking the fatal step.

'I wouldn't really know. I...I don't drink.' Another ruthless stance she'd taken since Greg. That last night before the police had crashed in and carted her away, he'd plied her with vintage champagne and caviar. She'd been so drunk she'd been barely coherent when her life had taken a nosedive into hell.

'My, what a virtuous life you lead, Moneypenny. Do you have any vices *at all*? Apart from your pancakes, that is?'

'None that I wish to divulge,' she responded before she managed to stop herself.

Sakis gave a low, rich laugh that soaked into her senses before fizzing pleasure along her nerve endings. 'I find that infinitely intriguing.' His gaze dropped to her mouth in a blatant, heated caress.

His lips parted and a slow rush of breath hissed through them. Slowly, almost leisurely, he stepped closer, bringing his body heat within singeing distance.

*Move, Brianna!*

Her feet finally heeded the frenzied warning fired by her brain but she'd barely taken a step when Sakis reached out. He caught her around the waist and brought her flush against him.

The contact fired through her, so powerful and potent, she lost her footing. One strong hand cupped her chin and raised her head to his merciless gaze. In his eyes, she read dangerous intent that made her stomach hollow with anticipation and feverish need, even as the last functioning brain cells shrieked for her to fight against the dangerous sensations.

'I'm going to kiss you now, Moneypenny,' Sakis breathed. 'It's not wise and it probably won't be safe.'

'Then you shouldn't do it…' She half-pleaded but already wet heat oozed between her thighs.

He gave a half-pained groan. 'I can't seem to stop myself.'

'Mr Pantelides—'

'Sakis. Say it. Say my name.'

She shook her head.

His head dropped another fraction. 'You're doing it again.'

'D-doing what?'

'Refusing to obey me.'

'We're no longer in the office.'

'Which is all the more reason why we should drop formalities. Say my name, Brianna.'

The way he said her name, the soft stresses on the vowels, made her insides clench hard. She tried desperately to fight against the overwhelming sensation. 'No.'

He walked her back until he had her pinned between the gym wall and the solid column of his hot body. The hard muscles of his bare chest were torture against her heavy breasts but it was the firm, unmistakeable imprint of his erection against her belly that made her stop breathing.

'Luckily for you, the need to taste you overwhelms the need to command your obedience.' His lips brushed hers in the fleetest of caresses. 'But I *will* hear you say it before very long.'

Eyelids too heavy to sustain fluttered downwards. Drowsy with lust, she fought to answer him. 'Don't count on it. I have a few rules of my own. This is one of them.'

The very tip of his tongue traced her lower lip,

again with the fleetest of touches, and the fiery blaze of need raged through her. 'What's another?'

'Not to get involved with the boss.'

'Hmm, that's one I agree with.'

'Then…what are you *doing*?' she asked plaintively.

'Proving that this isn't more than temporary insanity.' His voice reflected the dazed confusion she felt.

'Won't walking away prove the same thing? As you said, this might not be exactly wise.'

'Or this is nothing but a no-big-deal kiss. It'll only become a big deal if we aren't able to handle what happens afterwards.'

*No big deal.* Was it really? And would it hurt to experience just a kiss? They were both clothed… well, he was technically only half-clothed…but she could put the brakes on this any time she wanted… couldn't she?

'Afterwards?' she blurted.

'Yes, when we go back to what we are. You'll continue to be the aficionado who runs my business life and I'll be the boss who demands too much of you.'

'Or we could stop this right now. Pretend it never happened?'

A hard gleam entered his eyes. 'Pretence has

never been my style. I leave that to people who wish to hide their true colours; who want the world to perceive them as something other than what they are. I detest people like that, Moneypenny.' His mouth dropped another centimetre closer, his hands tightening around her waist as his eyes darkened with hot promise. 'It's why I won't pretend that the thought of kissing you, of being inside you, hasn't been eating me alive these past few days. It's also why I know neither of us will misconstrue this. Because you're above pretence. You're exactly who you say you are. Which is why I appreciate you so much.'

He kissed her then, his mouth devouring hers with a hunger so wild, so ferocious, it melted every single thought from her head.

Which was fortunate. Because otherwise she wouldn't have been able to stop herself from showing her reaction to his stark words; from blurting out that she was not even remotely who he thought she was.

# CHAPTER SIX

SAKIS FELT HER moan of desire shudder through her sexy body and groaned in return. *Theos*, he'd been so determined not to be seen by another woman in the work environment in the way that Giselle had portrayed him in court and in the media that he'd deliberately blinded himself to just how sexy, how utterly feminine and incredibly gorgeous, Brianna was. Now he let his reeling senses register her attributes—the hands' span soft but firm curve of her bare waist underneath his fingers; the saucy shape of her bottom and the way the supple globes felt in his hands.

And *Theos*, her mouth! Delicious and silky soft, it was pure torture just imagining it around the hard, stiff part of his anatomy. Sure enough, the image slammed into his brain, firing the mother lode of all sex bombs straight to his groin.

He wanted her with a depth that seriously disturbed him. He wanted her spread underneath him, naked and needy, in endless positions…

She gave a hitched cry as his tongue breached her sweet plump lips and mercilessly plunged in. He was being too rough. His brain fired at him to slow down but he couldn't pull back. He'd had a taste of her but somehow that first taste had demanded a second, a third…

He pressed down harder, demanding more of her. His hips ground into her lower body until he was fully cradled between her thighs but even that wasn't enough. His hands cupped her breasts and another shudder raked through her as his fingers tweaked her nipples. Blood roared through his ears at the thought of tasting them, of suckling them, tugging on them with his teeth.

When her hands finally rose to clutch his bare shoulders, when her nails dug into his skin, the rush of lust was so potent he feared he'd pass out there and then.

*What the hell was happening here?*

He'd never been this swept away by lust, even when he'd been in the clutches of his hormones as a young adult. Sex was great. He was a healthy, virile male who was rich and powerful enough to command the best female attention whether he wanted it or not. When he wanted it, he went all in for the enjoyment of it.

But never had he experienced this urgency, this slightly crazed need that threatened to take him out at the knees.

*And they hadn't even left first base yet!*

Brianna opened her mouth wider to accommodate his rough demand. One hand left his shoulder and plunged into his hair, scraping his scalp as her fingers tightened.

He welcomed the mild pain with a glee that seriously worried him.

He'd never gone for kinky but with every scrape of her fingers his erection grew harder, more painful. God, he was so turned on, he couldn't see straight.

Which was why it took a full minute to realise the fingers in his hair were pulling him back, not egging him on; that the hand on his shoulder was pushing him away with more than a little desperation.

'No!' The force of his kiss smothered the word but it finally penetrated his lust-engorged senses.

With a shocked groan, he lifted his head and staggered back.

Brianna stared up at him, her ragged breath rushing through lips swollen with the force of his kisses. But it was the expression in her turquoise eyes that froze his insides. Besides the shock mingled with arousal, the apprehension was back again.

Self-loathing ripped through him like a tornado. He might not have understood why she'd been terrified the first time, but this time he knew the blame lay squarely with him. He'd fallen on her like a horny barbarian.

He clenched his fists and took another step back. His chest rose and fell like a felon in the heat of pursuit and he dimly registered that he hadn't bothered to breathe since he'd first tasted her.

'I…think this has gone far enough,' she said, her eyes darkening as they fell to his chest and skittered away.

Sakis wanted to refute that, to growl that it hadn't gone far enough. But he would be speaking from the depths of whatever insanity gripped him.

*Insanity...*

Was that what he'd scornfully professed he wanted to test?

Well, now he knew. His gaze dropped to her mouth again and fresh need slammed into him.

Damn it… He *knew*, and yet he wanted more. Of course, 'more' was out of the question. Brianna held far more value to him as his assistant than she would as his lover.

Potential lovers were a dime a dozen. He only had to scroll through his diary…

The thought of doing just that for the sake of slaking the lust-monkey riding him made his mouth curl with distaste. He wasn't his father, taking and discarding women with barely a thought between incidents, not caring about who bore the brunt of his actions.

Sucking in another breath, he forced a nod.

'*Ne*, you're right.' He licked his lower lip, tasted her again and nearly groaned. He clawed a hand through his hair and fought to regain the control that had been all but non-existent since he walked into the gym, fully intent on a mind-clearing workout, only to find her contorted in a highly suggestive stretch that had fried his brain cells. 'Let's chalk it down to the pressure of the past seventy-two hours.'

A look passed through her eyes before her lids lowered. 'Is this how you normally deal with a crisis?'

He gave another tight smile, whirled away and came face to face with his image.

*Theos*, no wonder she was frightened.

He looked like a crazed animal, a monster with wild eyes burning with stark hunger and a raging hard-on. He kept his back to her then forced himself to answer evenly.

'No, I normally fly down to the lake and take a scull out on the water. Or I come here to the gym and use the rowing machine. Physical labour helps me work things through.' Unfortunately, the physical he had in mind now involved Brianna beneath him, her thighs spread out in response to his hard, demanding thrusts.

'Um…okay. I guess I was in your way, then. Shall I…let you get on with it?' The slight question in her tone demanded reassurance.

Sakis had none to give. He remained exactly where he was, his back to her as he willed his body under control.

'Mr Pantelides?'

He winced at the rigid formality in those two words. Gritting his teeth, he turned to face her. 'Don't worry, Moneypenny. Nothing's changed. You tasted sweet enough but this was nothing to lose my head over. Our little experiment is over. The board is reconvening at eight. I'll see you in the office at seven-thirty.'

A gym workout was now out of the question. Brianna's scent lingered in the air and threatened to mess with his mind.

'Okay. I'll see you in the morning, then. Goodnight, Mr—'

'*Kali nichta*, Moneypenny.' He cut her off before she could trot out his title again.

Sakis scooped up his shirt, thought about putting it back on and discarded the idea. Since he couldn't stay here, a two- — no, make that three-—mile swim in his pool was the next best option.

He was still staring at his shirt when she walked past him smelling of crushed lilies, rampant sex and sweat. God, what a combination. Against his will, his gaze tracked her sleek form. The taut, bare skin of her waist taunted him, as did the tight curve of her ass as she swayed her way out. With each sexy stride, the fire sweeping through his groin threatened to rage out of control.

It took a full minute after she'd left to realise he was still standing in the middle of the gym, clutching his shirt, gazing at the space where she'd been. With his fist tightening around the creased cotton, Sakis forced himself to admit that things indeed were about to get way worse before they got better.

And not just with his company.

*'You tasted sweet enough but this was nothing to lose my head over...'* Brianna forced herself to dwell on the relief rather than the sharp hurt bur-

rowing inside her. The dangerous theory had been tested, the fire had been breached and they'd come out unscathed.

*Are you sure?* Brianna kicked off her leotard with more force than was necessary. 'Yes, I'm sure,' she said out loud. 'One-hundred per cent sure,' she added for good measure.

Her top followed and she strode into the lavish cream-and-gold decorated bathroom. Turning on the shower, she stepped beneath the spray. Hot rivulets coursed over her face, over the mouth Sakis had devoured less than five minutes ago, and a fresh wave of desire rushed over her.

'No!' Her hands shook as she reached for the shower gel and spread it over her body. This wasn't happening. *But it was... It had...*

She'd let Sakis kiss her, had fallen into his hands like a ripe peach at harvest. She'd chosen to test the waters and had almost drowned in the process.

Because that kiss had rocked her to the depths of her soul. He'd kissed her like she was the last tangible thing in his universe, like he wanted to devour her. Aside from the pleasure of it, she'd felt his need as keenly as the need she'd fought so hard to suppress.

She didn't want to *need.* For as long as she could remember, needing had only brought her disaster.

As a child, her needs had come last for a mother who was only interested in her next drug fix. As a grown woman, she'd let her need for affection blind her into believing Greg's lies.

Nothing would make her return to that dark, *needful* place.

Her fingers drifted once again to her tattoo.

Whatever it was Sakis needed, he could find it elsewhere.

Sakis was already in the office when she arrived just before seven. He was on the phone but cool, green eyes skated over her as she entered. Replaying the pep talk she'd given herself before she'd come downstairs, she indicated his half-finished espresso cup and he nodded. The gaze that met hers as she stepped forward to pick up his cup was all ruthless business. There was no hint of the gritty, desire-ravaged man from the gym last night.

Sakis Pantelides, suave CEO and master of his world, was back in residence.

Brianna forced herself to emulate his expression as she walked out on decidedly shaky legs towards the state-of-the-art coffee machine in the little alcove just behind her office. Setting the cup beneath the stainless silver spouts, she pressed the button.

Last night's lurid dreams, which had kept her

tossing and turning in heated agitation, needed to be swept under the carpet of professionalism where they belonged. It was obvious Sakis had consigned the gym incident to 'done and forgotten'. She needed to do the same or risk—

'Is the machine delivering something other than coffee this morning? The daily horoscope, perhaps?' he drawled.

She whirled around. Sakis stood directly behind her, his powerful and overwhelming physique shrinking the space to even smaller proportions. 'I…sorry?'

His gaze flicked to the freshly made espresso and back to her face. 'The coffee is ready and yet you're staring at the machine as if you're expecting a crystal ball to materialise alongside the beverage.'

'Of course I wasn't. I was just…' She stopped, then with pursed lips picked up his cup and handed it to him. 'I wasn't that long, Mr Pantelides.'

His lips pursed at the use of his name but, now they were back in the work environment and back to being *professional*, he couldn't exactly object.

Expecting him to move, her heartbeat escalated when he stayed put, blocking her escape back to her office. 'Was there something else?'

His gaze dropped to her lips as he took a sip of his espresso. 'Did you sleep well?'

Unwanted flames licked at the muscles clenching in her belly. She wanted to tell him that how she slept was none of his business. But she figured answering him would make him get out of her way faster. 'I did. Thank you for asking.'

She waited. He didn't move. 'I didn't,' he rasped. 'Last night was the worst night's sleep I've had in a very long time.'

'Oh… Um…' She started to lick her lips, thought better of it and blew out a short breath instead. Seriously, she had to find a way to douse these supremely inconvenient flames that leapt inside her whenever he was near. 'It's been a stressful few days. It was bound to affect you in some way sooner or later.'

One corner of his mouth lifted. '*Ne*, I'm sure you're right.' Once again his gaze dragged over her mouth. The tingling of her lips almost made her rub her fingers over them, to do something to make it stop.

She clamped her hands round her middle instead. 'Was there something else you needed?'

He threw back the rest of the hot espresso and placed the cup on the counter. Several seconds passed in silence then he heaved a sigh. 'I'm…

sorry if I frightened you last night. I didn't mean to get so carried away.'

Brianna's breath caught. 'I wasn't… You didn't…' She stopped speaking, her senses clamouring a warning as he stepped closer.

'Then why did you look so scared? Has someone hurt you in the past?'

She meant to say no, to diffuse the highly inquisitive gleam in his eyes before it got out of hand. But… 'Haven't we all been hurt at some point by someone we trusted? Someone we thought loved us?' Her stark answer hung in the air between them.

He paled a little, the lines bracketing his mouth deepening. 'I hope I didn't remind you of this person.'

'Not any more than I reminded you of your father.'

Her breath caught in her chest as anguish etched into his face. Until two days ago, she'd only known him to display the utmost control when it came to matters of business. Except this wasn't business. This was intensely private and intensely painful. Witnessing his raw pain made the ice surrounding her heart crack. Before she knew it, her hands were loosening and she was reaching for his arm.

She stopped herself just in time. 'Sorry, I didn't mean to bring that up.'

His smile was grim as his fingers clawed through his hair. 'Unfortunately, memories once resurrected aren't easy to dismiss, no matter how inconvenient the timing.'

'Is there ever a convenient time to dredge up past hurt?' Pain ripped through her question.

He heard it and froze. Green eyes speared hers in a look so intense her heart stuttered. 'Who hurt you, Brianna?' he asked again softly.

Feeling herself floundering, she sagged against the counter for support. 'I…this isn't really a topic for the office.'

*'Who?'* he insisted.

'You had problems with your father. Mine was with my mother.' Her voice sounded reedy, fraught with the anguish raking through her.

His smile held no mirth. 'Look at us: a pair of hopeless cases with mummy and daddy issues. Think what a field day psychologists would have with us.'

Not once in the past eighteen months had she believed she had anything in common with Sakis. But hearing his words brought a curious balm to her pain.

'Maybe we should ask for a group discount?' She attempted her own smile.

His eyes darkened then the pain slowly faded, to be replaced by another look, one she was becoming intimately familiar with. 'Was there a reason you came looking for me?' she asked a third time.

Sakis's jaw tightened. 'The investigators have confirmed there's a connection between the crash and the takeover.'

'Really?'

He nodded. 'It's highly suspect that a day after my tanker crashes Moorecroft Oil and Landers Petroleum make a bid for my company.' He turned and headed back into his office. 'Their timing was a little too precise for it to be opportunistic.'

She entered his office in time to see him snatch up his phone. 'Sheldon.' He addressed his head of security. 'I need you to dig deeper into Moorecroft Oil and Landers Petroleum.'

At the mention of Landers, Brianna froze. Thankfully, her ringing phone gave her the perfect excuse to return to her desk.

When Sakis emerged, she'd found some semblance of control, enough to accompany him into the board meeting without giving the state of her agitation away.

The conference call to Richard Moorecroft descended into chaos less than five minutes after Sakis had him on the line.

'How dare you accuse me of such a preposterous thing, Pantelides? You think I would stoop so low as to sabotage your vessel in order to achieve my ends?'

'You haven't achieved anything except draw attention to your own devious dealings.' A note of disdain coated Sakis's voice. 'Did you really think I'd roll over like a puppy because of one mishap?'

'You underestimate the might of Moorecroft. I'm a giant in the industry—'

'The fact that you feel the need to point that out impresses me even less.'

A huff of rage came over the conference line. 'This isn't over, Pantelides. You can count on it.'

'You're right, this isn't over. As we speak, I'm digging up any connection between what happened to my tanker and your company.'

'You won't find any!' The bravado in Moorecroft's voice was tinged with a shadowy nervousness that made Sakis's eyes gleam.

'Pray that I don't. Because, if I do, you can rest assured that I *will* come after you. And I won't be satisfied until I rip your precious company to little pieces and feed them to my pet piranhas.' The menace in his voice made ice crawl over Brianna's skin. 'And any accomplices will not be spared either.'

He stabbed the 'end' button and glanced around the other members of his board. 'I'll apprise you of any news if the investigation reaps any information.'

Sakis turned to where Brianna sat three seats to his left. He'd deliberately placed her out of his eyeline so she wouldn't prove a distraction. Not that he hadn't noticed her tapping away all during the conference. Now that he'd let himself experience the power of his attraction for her, he noticed everything about her. From the way her sleek, navy designer skirt hugged her bottom, to the arch of her feet when she walked into his presence.

At the most inappropriate times he'd caught himself wondering how long her hair was, whether it would feel soft and silky. Many times during his sleepless night, he'd pictured himself kissing her again, imagining the many ways he'd explore her lips again given another chance.

Only now, he noticed a little bit more. Like the vulnerability she tried to hide beneath the brusque exterior. Whatever her mother had done to her still had the power to wound her. His chest tightened with the need to go to her, brush his knuckles down her cheek and reassure her that he would take care of her…

*Theos!*

With gritted teeth, he tried to pull himself back under control. There would be no reassuring, just as there would be no repeat of last night's events. What happened in his gym last night couldn't be allowed to happen again.

Absolutely, without a shadow of a doubt.

So why was he walking towards her, letting his gaze devour the exposed line of her neck as she bent over her tablet? Why was he imagining himself lifting her up from that chair, sliding that tight skirt up—did she favour garter belts or thigh-high stockings?—and bending her over his boardroom table?

*Stasi.*

He was losing it and it wasn't even nine o'clock in the morning! With a curt command, he dismissed his board members.

He waited until the room cleared before he murmured her name.

She lifted her head and stared straight at him. Deep turquoise eyes met his and Sakis wasn't sure whether the interest it held was personal or professional. That he couldn't even read her properly any more, sent a fizz of annoyance through him.

'So, what happens now? I didn't think you'd let Moorecroft know we were investigating his connection with the tanker.'

Stopping a mere foot from her, he shrugged. 'I called his bluff and it paid off. I wasn't sure until I heard it in his voice. He's involved.'

'Then why not go after him?'

'He knows he's cornered. Between the FCA investigation and my own, he'll either come clean or he'll try to do whatever he can to cover his tracks. Either way, his time is fast running out. I'll give him a few hours to decide which way he wants to go.'

'And if he reveals a connection?'

Sakis heard the tremble in her voice and wondered at it.

'Then I'll make sure he pays to the fullest extent.' His father had got away with shady business deals for a long time before he'd been brought to justice. The same newspapers that had uncovered his treachery had uncovered the many families and employees his father had duped out of their rightful rewards.

Once his father had been put behind bars and Ari had been old enough to take over the reins of the company, the first thing he'd done was make sure the affected families were recompensed.

Letting anyone get away with fraud and duplicity would never happen.

He glanced down into the face of the woman whose body had invaded his dreams last night. She'd paled considerably, her eyes wide and haunted. His frown deepened.

'What's wrong?'

She surged to her feet and started gathering her things. 'Nothing.'

'Wait.' He placed a halting hand on her waist and immediately felt her tense. Another stream of irritation rushed upward.

'Y-yes?' Her voice wasn't quite steady and her head was bent, hiding her expression.

'Brianna, what's the hell is going on?'

'Why should there be anything wrong? I'm merely returning to my office to get on with the rest of the day.' Her words emerged in a rush.

Something was definitely wrong; something he'd said. He replayed his last words in his head, then his lips pursed.

'You think my views are too harsh?'

Her mouth tightened but she still avoided eye contact. 'What does it matter what I think?'

'Tell me, what would you do?' His hand curved firmly around her waist. When she moved, he felt the warm softness beneath his fingers. He wanted to pull her closer, glide his hand upward and cup her breast the way he had last night. It took every single ounce of willpower for him to hold himself still.

'I…I would listen to them, find out the motive behind their actions first, before I throw them to the wolves.'

'Greed is greed. Betrayal is betrayal. The reason for it ceases to matter once the act is done.'

Her soft lips pursed. Her nostrils flared and Sakis caught a sense of anger bubbling beneath her skin. 'If you truly believe that, then I don't see the point of you asking me.'

'Under what circumstances would you forgive such an action?'

She gave a small shrug. The movement drew his attention to her breast. Sakis swallowed and cursed the heat flaring through his groin. 'If the act was done to protect someone you cared about. Or perhaps it was done without the perpetrator knowing he was committing an act of betrayal.'

Sakis's lips twisted. 'My father's betrayal was an active undertaking. So is Moorecroft's.'

Her eyes clashed with his then she glanced away. 'You can't assign your father's sins to every situation in your life, Mr Pantelides.'

This was getting personal again. But he couldn't

seem to stop himself from spilling the jagged pain in his chest. 'My father actively cheated and bribed his way through his business dealings for decades. He betrayed his family over and over, letting us think he was one thing when he was in fact another. Even after he was found out, he was remorseless. Even jail didn't change him. He went to his grave unrepentant.' He sucked in a breath and forcibly steered his thoughts away from the bitterness of his past. 'You're deluding yourself if you think there's such as a thing as blind, harmless betrayal.'

A shaft of pain and sympathy flitted through her eyes, just like it had back at Point Noire. She even started to move towards him before she visibly stopped herself.

Sakis felt curiously bereft that she succeeded.

'I'm sorry for what happened to you. I…I have emails to catch up on so, if you don't mind, I'll get back to the office.'

'No.'

She stared at him in surprise. 'No?'

He glanced at his watch. 'You haven't had breakfast yet, have you?'

'No, but I was going to order some fruit and cereal from the kitchen.'

'Forget that. We're going out.'

'I don't see why—'

'I do. We've both been cooped up in here since yesterday. Some fresh air and a proper meal will do us some good. Come.' He started to walk out and felt a hint of satisfaction when after several seconds he heard her footsteps behind him.

Sakis took her to a café on a quiet street in Cheapside. The manager greeted him with a smile and offered them a red high-backed booth set back from the doorway. One look at the menu and her eyes flew to collide with Sakis's.

He was regarding her with a seriously sexy smile on his face.

'All they serve here are pancakes,' she blurted.

'I know, which is why I brought you here. Time to indulge that *weakness* of yours.' The way he stressed the word made a spike of heat shoot through her.

'But...why?' Frantically, she scrambled to gather her rapidly unravelling control. Far from being back on the professional footing she'd thought, the morning was turning into one huge, personal landmine. One she wasn't sure she would survive.

'Because it's perfect ammunition.' Again he smiled and her heart lurched.

'You see my weakness for pancakes as *ammunition*?' She felt her lips twitch and allowed herself a small smile. Just then, a waiter walked past with a steaming heap of blueberry pancakes dripping in honey. She barely managed to stifle her groan, but Sakis heard it.

A dark, hungry look entered his eyes that made her stomach muscles clench hard. 'I'm not so sure whether to be pleased or irritated that I've uncovered this piece of information about you, Brianna. On the one hand, it could be the perfect weapon to get you to do whatever I want.'

'I already do whatever you want.' The loaded answer made heat crawl up her neck. His keen gaze followed it then scoured her face before locking on hers.

'Do you? I distinctly recall a few times when you've refused to do my bidding.'

'I wouldn't have lasted two minutes if I'd pandered to you in any shape or form.'

'No, you wouldn't have. I told Ari you were my Rottweiler.'

She gave a shocked gasp. 'You compared me to a dog?'

He grimaced and had the grace to look uncomfortable. 'It was a metaphor but, in hindsight, I should've used a more…flattering description.' He beckoned the waiter who'd been hovering a booth away.

Her curiosity got the better of her. 'How would you describe me?'

He didn't answer immediately. Instead he gave the waiter their order—coffee and two helpings of blueberry pancakes.

Brianna stopped the waiter with a hand on his arm. 'Can I have a side-helping of blueberries, please? And a bowl of honey? Oh, and some icing sugar and fresh cream…and two wedges of lemon…and some butter…' She stopped when she saw Sakis's eyebrow quirk in deep amusement. She dropped her arm and this time was unable to stop her blush from suffusing her face as their waiter walked away. 'Sorry, I didn't mean to sound like a complete glutton.'

'Don't apologise for your desires. Indulging every now and then is completely human.'

'Until I have to pay for it with hours in the gym. Then I'll hate every single mouthful I'm about to take.'

Immediately her mind homed in on what had happened between them last night. From the way his green eyes darkened, he was remembering too. God, what was wrong with her? Or maybe that was the wrong question. She knew what was wrong. Despite cautioning herself against it, she was attracted to Sakis with a fierce compulsion that defied reason. She accepted that now. What she needed was a cure for this insanity before it raged out of control.

'If you regret the act before it's happened, you take away the enjoyment of it.'

'So you're saying I should just ignore what will come afterwards and just live in the moment?'

His gaze dropped to her lips, the heat of it almost a caress that made her want to moan. 'Exactly.' He breathed the word then said nothing else.

Silence grew between them, the only sound the distant clatter of plates and cutlery from other diners.

She could only stand it for a few minutes until she felt as if she'd combust from the sizzling tension in the air. Forcefully, she cleared her throat and searched for a neutral subject, one that would defuse the stressful atmosphere. 'You were going to tell me what your description of me would be.' *Oh, nice one, Brianna.*

He sat back in his seat, extended his arm along the back of the booth. Her eyes fell on rippling muscle beneath his shirt and she barely managed to swallow.

'Perhaps now is not the time, or the place.'

*Leave it, Brianna...leave it.* 'Oh, is it that bad?'

'No, it's that *good*.'

She breathed deeply and opted for silence. When their food arrived, she pounced on it, feeding her culinary appetite the way she couldn't let herself feed on the dark, carnal promise in Sakis's eyes.

She looked up several minutes later to find him watching her with an expression of mingled shock and amusement.

'Sorry, it's your fault. Now you've unleashed my innermost craving, there's no stopping me.' She took another sinful bite and barely managed to stop her eyes rolling in pleasure.

'On the contrary, seeing you eat something other than a salad and with such…relish is a pleasurable experience in itself.'

'Don't worry; I'm not going to re-enact a *When Harry Met Sally* moment.'

A puzzled frown marred his forehead. 'A what?'

She laughed. 'You've never seen that clip where the actress simulates an orgasm in a restaurant?'

He swallowed. 'No, I haven't. But I prefer my orgasmic experiences not to be simulated. When it comes to orgasms, only the real thing will do. Do you not agree?'

Dear Lord, was she really having breakfast with her boss, discussing orgasms? 'I wasn't… This was…' She stopped, silently willing her racing pulse to quieten. 'I was merely making conversation. I don't have an opinion on orgasms one way or another.'

His low laugh caressed her senses like soft butterfly wings. '*Everyone* has an opinion on orgasms, Brianna. Some of us may have stronger opinions than others, but we all have them.'

She was not going to think about Sakis and orgasms together. *She was not.* 'Um…okay; point taken. But I'd rather not discuss it any longer, if that's okay with you?'

He finished the last of his pancakes and picked up his black coffee. 'Certainly. But some subjects have a habit of lingering until they're dealt with.'

'And other subjects deserve more attention than others. What was your other point?'

'Sorry?'

'Before the subject went…sideways you said "on the one hand". I was wondering what the other was.'

It was a purely diversionary tactic, but she wanted—no, needed—to get off the subject that was making desire dredge through her pelvis like a pervasive drug, threatening to fool her into thinking she could taste the forbidden and come out whole.

There would be no coming out whole once she gave in to the hunger that burned within her, that burned relentlessly in Sakis's eyes. Wanting—or, God forbid, *needing*—a man like Sakis would destroy her eventually. Their conversation in the boardroom had reiterated the fact that he was emotionally scarred from what his father had done to him. He would never allow himself to trust anyone, never mind reaching the point of *needing* another human being to the extent she suspected she would crave if she didn't control her feelings.

'On the other hand, I'm glad I know this weakness. Because I have a feeling you don't give yourself permission enough to enjoy the simple things in life.'

Her heart hammered with something suspiciously like elation. 'And you…you want to give me that?'

'I want to give you that. I want to indulge you like you've never been indulged before.'

Simple words. But oh, so dangerous to her current state of mind.

'Why?' she blurted before she could stop herself.

Her question seemed to surprise him. His lashes swept down and veiled his eyes. 'For starters, I'm hoping to be rewarded with one of those rare smiles of yours.' He looked back up and his expression stopped her breath. There was a solemn kinship, a gentleness in their depths, that made her heart flip. 'And because I had my brothers while I dealt with my daddy issues. But you, as far as I know, are an only child, correct?'

Emotion clogged her throat. 'Correct,' she croaked, battling the threat of tears.

That weird connection tightened, latched and embedded deeply, frightening but soothing at the same time. 'Let's call this therapy, then.' He glanced down at her plate where one last square of honey-soaked pancake was poised on her fork. 'Are you finished?'

She hadn't but the thought of putting that last morsel in her mouth while he watched with those all-seeing eyes was too much to bear. 'Yes, I'm done. And thank you…for this, I mean. And for…' She stumbled to a halt, alien feelings rushing through her at dizzying speed.

He nodded, stood and held out his hand. 'It was my pleasure, *agapita*.'

By the time they returned to the office, Brianna knew something had fundamentally changed between them. She didn't even bother to figure out a way back to equanimity; she couldn't. Curiously, she didn't feel as devastated at losing that particular battle.

It helped that they were barely in the door when

Sakis threw out a list of things he wanted her to do but, despite the breakneck speed of dealing with his demands, they were soon both plugged into events at Point Noire, especially the clean-up process and the still missing Pantelides Six crew-members.

After speaking to Morgan Lowell's wife Perla for the fifth time at six o'clock, Sakis threw his pen on his desk and ran both hands over his stubbled jaw.

'Are you okay?'

Tired eyes trained on her with breath-stopping intensity.

'I need to get out of here,' he rasped as he strode to the door and shrugged into his designer over-coat.

She swallowed and nodded. 'Do you want me to book a restaurant table for you? Or call a friend to...um...' She stopped, purely because the thought of arranging a date for Sakis with one of the many women who graced his electronic diary stuck in her gut like a sharp knife.

'I'm not in the mood to listen to inane conversation about the latest Hollywood gossip or who is screwing whom in my circle of friends.'

His response pleased her way more than it should have. 'Okay, what can I do?'

His eyes gleamed for a moment, before he looked

away and headed towards the door. 'Nothing.' He stopped with a hand on the door. 'I'm meeting Ari for a drink. And you're logging off for the night. Is that clear, Moneypenny?'

She nodded slowly and watched him walk out, hollowness in her stomach that made her hate herself. She wanted to be with him. She wanted to be the one who wiped away that look of weariness she'd seen in his eyes. And all through today, every time he'd called her 'Moneypenny', she'd wanted to beg him to call her 'Brianna'. Because she loved the way he said her name.

She glanced down at the fingers resting on her keyboard and wasn't surprised to see them trembling. Her whole being trembled with the depth of the feelings that had been coursing through her all day. Frankly, it scared the hell out of her.

Hurriedly, she shut down the computer and gathered her tablet, phone and handbag. She'd just slid her chair neatly into the space beneath her desk when the phone rang. Thinking it was Sakis—because who else would ring her at seven-thirty on a work night?—she pounced on the handset.

'Hello?'

'May I speak to Anna Simpson?'

A spear of ice pinned her in place as her lips parted on a soundless gasp. A full minute passed.

Her lungs burned until she managed to force herself back from the brink of unconsciousness. 'Excuse me, I…I think you've got the wrong number.'

The ugly laugh at the end of the line shook her to the very soul. 'We both know I don't have the wrong number, don't we, sweetheart?

She didn't respond—couldn't—because the phone had fallen from her nerveless fingers.

Another full minute passed. 'Hello?' came the impatient echoing voice. 'Anna?'

Numbness spreading through her, she picked up the phone. 'I told you there…there's no one by that name working here.'

But it was too late. She recognised the taunting, reedy voice at the end of the line. It was a voice she'd been dreading hearing again since her return from Point Noire.

'I can play along if you prefer, Anna. Hell, I'll even call you by your new name, *Brianna Moneypenny.* But we both know to me you'll always be Anna, don't we?' mocked Greg Landers.

## CHAPTER SEVEN

'WHAT DO YOU want, Greg?' Brianna snapped into her mobile phone as she threw her bag on the tiny sofa in her small living room.

'What? No hello, no pleasantries? Never mind. I'm glad you were sensible enough to return my call. Although, I don't get why you didn't want to speak to me at your office. I made sure Pantelides wasn't there before I called.'

Shock made her grip the edge of the seat. 'You're having him watched?'

'No, I'm having *you* watched. You're the one I'm interested in.'

*'Me?'*

'Yes. For now, at least. Tell me, why the name change?'

Bitterness rose in a sweltering tide, bringing a sickening haze that made the furnishings of her small flat blur. 'Why the hell do you think? You destroyed my life, Greg. After you lied and swore under oath in court that I embezzled funds from your company, when we both know that it was you who set up that Cayman Islands account in my name. Do you think after what you put me through anyone would've hired me once they knew I'd been to prison for embezzlement?'

'Tsk-tsk, let's not blow things out of proportion, shall we? You served well under half of the four-year prison term. If it's any consolation, I only expected you to get a slap on the wrist.'

'It's *not* a consolation!'

'Besides,' he continued as if she hadn't interrupted, 'I hear those prisons are just a step down from glorified holiday camps.'

The scar on her hip—the result of a shiv, courtesy of an inmate whose attention she wouldn't return—burned at the careless dismissal of what had been a horrific period of her life. 'It's a shame you decided not to try it out for yourself, then, instead of turning coward and letting someone else take the blame for your greed. Now, are you going to tell me what this call is about or shall I hang up?'

'Hang up and I'll make sure your salacious past is the first thing Pantelides reads about when he steps into that ivory tower of his tomorrow morning.'

Brianna's hand tightened around the phone at the ruthless tone. 'How did you find me, anyway?'

Not that it mattered now. But she'd used every last penny to erase her past, to make sure every trace of Anna Simpson was wiped clean as soon as she'd attained her freedom.

'I didn't. *You* found *me*, through the wonderful medium of TV. Imagine my surprise when I tuned in, like every environmentally conscious individual out there who's horrified about the Pantelides oil spillage, to find you right behind the main man himself. It took me a few minutes to recognise you, though. I much prefer you blonde to the brunette you used to be. Which is the real thing?'

'I fail to see…' She stopped because the Greg she'd known, the man she'd once foolishly thought herself in love with, hadn't changed. He believed himself a witty and clever conversationalist and was never one to get to the point until he was ready. It was one of the things—many things, she realised now—that had irritated her about him. 'Blonde is my natural colour.'

Greg sighed. 'Such a shame you chose to wear that dull brown when I knew you. Maybe I'd have thought twice before taking the route I took.'

'No, you wouldn't have. Your slimy nature makes you interested in taking care of number one. Are you going to tell me what you want any time soon?'

'You're distressed so I'll let that insult slide. But be careful now or I'll forget my manners. Now, what do I want? It's very simple: I want Pantelides Shipping. And you're going to help me get it.'

*You're out of your mind* was the first of many outraged responses that rushed into her head. She managed to stop herself before they spilled out. Slowly, she sank onto her sofa, the only piece of furniture in her living room aside from a lone coffee table, as her mind raced.

'And why would I do that?'

'To protect your dirty little secret, of course.'

She licked her lips as fear threatened to swamp any semblance of clear thinking. 'What makes you think my boss doesn't already know?'

'Don't take me for a fool, Anna.'

'My name is Brianna.' The woman Greg thought he knew no longer existed.

'If you want to keep calling yourself that, you'll give me what I want. And don't bother telling me Pantelides knows about your past. He's scrupulous when it comes to any hint of scandal. You're the last person he'd employ if he knew your past was as shady as his father's.'

This time her gasp was audible. It echoed around the room in tones of pain, shock and anger. 'You know about his father?'

'I do my homework, sweetheart. And if he'd bothered to do his he'd have discovered who you really were. But I'm glad he didn't, because now you're in the perfect position to help me.'

The vice tightened harder around her chest. 'What exactly is it you want me to do?'

'I need information. As much as you can get your hands on. Specifically, which of the board members hold the largest shares, aside from Pantelides. And which of the other members will be amenable to selling what shares they have.'

'You know this will never work, don't you? Sakis—Mr Pantelides—will crush you if you come within a whisper of his company.'

'God, you haven't gone and done it again, have you, Anna?' came the soft taunt.

Brianna shivered. 'Done what?'

'Offered that foolish little heart of yours on a silver platter to another boss?' he murmured in a pitying voice.

'I don't know what you're talking about.' But deep down there was no hiding from the truth. Her feelings for Sakis had morphed from purely professional to something else. Something she was vehemently unwilling to examine right now, when she needed all her wits about her to defend herself against what her grimy ex was intent on pulling her into.

'You have four days, Anna. I'll be in touch and I expect you to have the information I need.'

Her mouth went dry. Her heart hammered with sick fear and loathing and the unmistakeable, sinking feeling of inevitability. 'And if I don't?'

'Then your boss will wake up to a most tantalising double-page spread of his treasured assistant in the tabloid press on Saturday morning. I'm pretty sure with very little effort I can get Pantelides Shipping to start trending again on all social media.'

Her belly quivered and she clenched her muscles hard. 'Why are you doing this? Haven't you done enough? Aren't the millions you squirrelled away enough?'

'Every Joe Bloggs knows how to make a million these days. No, sweetheart, my ambitions are set much higher than that. I'd hoped my association with Moorecroft would see me there but the fool folded at the first sign of adversity. Fortunately, I have you now.'

'I haven't agreed to anything.'

'But you will. You covet your position almost as much as I covet the prospect of acquiring Pantelides Shipping. Make no mistake, I will have it.'

'Greg—'

'I'll be in touch on Friday. Don't disappoint me, Anna.'

He hung up before she could appeal to his better nature. Who was she kidding? Greg had no better nature. He was a vulture who ruthlessly fed on the weak.

The discovery that he'd engineered her to take the fall for his failing company over three years ago had rocked her to the core. When he'd pleasantly asked her to act as his co-director, she'd thought nothing of it, especially when he'd brought in a legal expert to explain things to her. Of course, it'd turned out the so-called legal expert had been in on the scheme to bleed his company dry before declaring bankruptcy and leaving her to take the fall.

She'd had time to dwell on her stupidity and gullibility in the maximum-security prison the judge had sentenced her to, to set an example.

Brianna staggered up from the sofa, swaying on shaky legs as her mind spun with the impossibility of her situation.

The very idea of betraying Sakis made her stomach turn over in revulsion.

He would never forgive her if she brought his company under unpalatable scrutiny so soon after his tanker's crash and having the memory of his father resurrected.

She could resign with immediate effect. But what would stop Greg from spewing his vitriol purely out of spite?

Telling Sakis the truth was out of the question.

*Betrayal is betrayal. The reason for it ceases to matter once the act is done.*

Casting her gaze around the almost empty room, another shiver raked through her.

*Run!*

The stark reality of her harsh childhood had made it impossible for her to fully imbed herself in any one place, even this place she called her sanctuary. At least, if she had to run, she could be out of here in less than half an hour.

She pressed her lips together as a spike of rebellion clayed her feet. Why should she run? She'd done nothing wrong. Her only folly had been to delude herself into thinking Greg cared for her. But she'd paid the price for it.

No more. *No more!*

Throwing down the mobile phone, she went into her equally sparsely furnished bedroom. The bed lay on wooden slats on the floor. Aside from a super-sized *papier-mâché* cat she'd bought at a Sunday market months ago, only a tall, broad-leafed ficus plant graced the room. Her only indulgence was the luxury cashmere throw and the fluffy pillows on the bed. Even the built-in wardrobe held only the collection of designer suits Sakis had insisted she used her expense account for when she'd joined Pantelides Shipping. Her own clothes consisted of a few pairs of jeans and tops, one set of jogging bottoms and jumper and two pairs of trainers.

*Those would be easy to pack.*

No; she refused to think like a fugitive. She had nothing to be ashamed of.

With shaky fingers, she undressed and entered the *en suite* bathroom, suddenly eager to wash away the grime of her conversation with Greg. But his threat lingered in the air, in the water. No matter how much she scrubbed, she felt tainted by the thought that she had even contemplated betrayal to save her own skin.

The pounding at her door finally registered over the hammering of her heart and the rush of the shower. Twisting the tap shut, she heard the faint sound of her mobile just before another round of hammering made her lunge for her dressing down. With a quick sluice of a towel over her body, she went to her door and peered through the peephole.

The massive frame of Sakis looming through the

distorted glass quickly eroded the relief that Greg hadn't found his way to her flat.

It seemed the two people responsible for the angst in her life were determined to breach her sanctuary at all costs today.

Pulse skittering out of control, Brianna cracked open the door. 'I...I didn't know you knew where I lived.' She looked into his clenched-jawed face and her words died on her lips. 'Why are you here?'

'I came here because...' He stopped, then clawed a hand through his hair. 'Hell, I'm not exactly sure why I came here. But I know I didn't want to be at the penthouse by myself.' He raked his hand through his hair again. The weariness she'd glimpsed on his face earlier seemed amplified a hundred-fold. The soft place inside her chest that had been expanding since their pancake episode this morning widened even further and she found herself stepping back.

'I... Would you like to come in?'

Lips pursed, he nodded. Standing to one side in the narrow hallway, she held her breath as he entered her sanctuary.

Immediately, he dwarfed the space. She shut the door and entered the living room to find him pacing the space in short, jerky strides.

'Can I get you a drink?' She hadn't touched the

bottle of scotch that had come with her Christmas hamper last year. Now she was grateful for it as she produced the bottle and Sakis nodded.

She took out a glass, poured a healthy measure and passed it to him.

'Aren't you having one?' Despite his question, his gaze was focused on the amber liquid in his hand.

'I don't really…' She stopped. After what she'd been through already tonight, what she sensed was coming, perhaps a small drink wouldn't hurt. She poured a single shot for herself, took a sip and nearly choked as the liquid burned a fiery path through her chest.

With a grim smile, Sakis tossed his own drink back in one unflinching gulp. He set his glass down on the coffee table and faced her.

'Why did you leave?'

The reason for returning home blazed at the back of her mind. Although she'd done nothing wrong, guilt clawed through her nevertheless. She licked her lips then froze when his eyes darkened. 'I haven't been home in a while. I just wanted to touch base.'

'And touching base precluded you from answering your phone?'

She glanced at the phone she'd abandoned on

the sofa after her call with Greg. Picking it up, she activated it and saw twelve missed calls on the screen.

'Sorry, I was in the shower.'

His agitated pacing brought him closer. He stopped a couple of feet from her. But the distance meant nothing because she could feel the heat of his body reaching out, caressing her, claiming her. Tendrils of damp hair that had escaped the knot clung to her nape, sending tiny rivulets of water down her back. Supremely conscious that she was naked beneath her gown, she tried to take a step back but her feet were frozen on the carpet.

His gaze traced over her and stopped at the rapid rise and fall of her chest. She watched his fists clench and release as stark hunger transformed his face into a mesmerising mask.

'I'm sorry to have disturbed you,' he rasped, but nothing in his tone or his face showed contrition. Instead, his stare intensified, whipping the air around her until a helpless moan escaped her lips.

Abandoning reason, Brianna stepped closer, bringing her body flush against his. Knowing she risked betraying her very soul, but unable to stop herself, she cupped his jaw. 'You ordered me to stop working. I didn't think you'd need me tonight.'

Her breath caught as his gaze moved hungrily over her lips.

'No, Brianna. Far from it. I need you. More now than I've ever needed you before. You're the only one who makes the world make sense to me.'

'I…I am?'

'*Ne*. I didn't like it when I couldn't reach you.' His head dropped a fraction until his forehead touched hers. 'I can't function without you by my side.'

'I'm here now,' she whispered, her throat clogged with emotions she couldn't give name to. No, scratch that: it was desire, passion and compassion all rolled into one needful and relentless ache. That visceral need to connect with Sakis that she'd never felt with anyone else, not even her own mother. 'Whatever you need, I'm here.'

One hand fisted her damp, precariously knotted hair, pulling it back almost roughly so her face was tilted up and exposed to his. 'Are you?' he enquired roughly.

She gave a shaky nod. 'Yes.'

'Be very sure, *glikia mou*. Because this time I won't be able to stop. If you don't want me to go any further, tell me now.' His eyes searched her urgently, his need clearly displayed in the harsh whistle of breath that escaped his parted lips.

The hard body plastered to hers made thinking near impossible but Brianna knew one thing—this could be her one chance to be with Sakis. After Friday, she'd be out of a job—one she would be sacked from or have to resign from.

From a purely selfish point of view, this could be her last chance to experience the fervid promise of bliss she'd felt in the gym last night—to be bold enough to reach for something she'd once dared to crave.

'Brianna?' His fierce tone held a hint of vulnerability that struck deep.

Sakis needed her. And she…she needed to blank out the heartache the future held.

'Yes, I want you…'

He swallowed the words with the savage demand of his kiss. The hand at her waist lowered to grasp her bottom and he pulled her into stinging contact with his groin, giving a low groan as the force of his erection probed her belly.

For an endless age, he devoured her mouth with a hunger born of desperation. Brianna gave as much as she got, her hunger just as maddeningly urgent. When his tongue curled around hers, she opened her mouth wider to feel even more of it.

Sakis groaned again and walked her back until the back of her legs touched her small sofa. He'd barely pushed her down before he covered her with his immense body. Searing heat engulfed her as they lay plastered from chest to thigh. Raising his head, his gaze scoured her face as if imprinting her features on his memory. When it touched her lips, the urge to lick them overcame her. She passed her tongue over them and watched in secret delight as his eyes darkened dramatically.

'I suspected that underneath those severe business suits you were a seductress, Moneypenny.'

'I'm sure I have no idea what you mean.' She licked her lips again.

His growl was her first warning but she was too far gone to heed it.

Brianna quickly pulled his head down and brushed his lips with hers. She kissed him again and felt her heart leap with joy when he deepened it.

When he suddenly surged off her and stood, Brianna fought not to cry out in disappointment. But he merely shrugged out of his jacket and tie before plucking her off the seat. 'I'm so lucky to have you. But my gratitude does not extend to making love to you on a sofa made for elves.'

'Oh. I guess it is a little on the small side, isn't it?'

'Perhaps not, if you're trying to be inventive. We'll leave it for another time.'

The thrill that went through her escalated when he caught her up in his arms and took her lips in another searing kiss. 'Which way to the bedroom?'

Brianna pointed and he immediately steered her in that direction. At the door, she hesitated. What would he think when he saw how sparsely decorated her room was? She was scrambling to think of excuses when he pulled her hips into his groin.

'I don't mind doing it standing up if that's what you'd prefer, *glikia mou*. Just say the word,' he breathed against her neck, one hand sneaking up to cup her bare breast where her gown had fallen open. With another groan, he squeezed before teasing the nub between his fingers. 'But say it quickly before I combust from neglect.'

'The...the bedroom is fine.' She opened the door and held her breath. But Sakis was only interested in the bed, not the state of the near-empty room. He propelled her firmly towards it, shucking off his shoes, socks and shirt without letting go completely. With a firm hand he pushed her onto the bed and fell onto his knees behind her.

Pulling her back, he ground his hips into her. 'You have no idea how many times I've imagined you in this position before me.' Urgent hands slid up her dressing gown and he growled with ragged need as he bared her naked bottom to his heated gaze. '*Theos*, no knickers. This is even better than I imagined.' Roughly, he reached for the sleeves of the gown and jerked it off her completely.

Brianna was thankful she wasn't facing him so that she didn't have to explain her tattoo to him just yet, especially since, with the depth of her need, she wasn't sure she wouldn't blurt out the truth behind it. The other thing was her scar. She couldn't hide it for ever but she was grateful she didn't have to explain it right this minute.

Because the sensation of Sakis touching her naked bottom, caressing and decadently moulding it, made her senses melt.

'*Theos*, I love your ass,' he growled with dirty reverence.

Pure feminine delight fizzed through her. 'I can tell,' she responded breathily.

His laugh was low and deep, doing nothing to disguise his hunger. She jerked with surprise and delight when she felt his mouth touch each globe in an open-mouthed kiss before biting lightly on her flesh.

He continued to knead her with his large hands, massaging down to her hips before returning to fondle her with both hands. The eroticism of the act made her breath catch. But it was when he pushed her forward and spread apart her thighs that she stopped breathing.

Sakis blew a hot breath on her parted folds, making her thighs quiver in anticipation of what was to come. When it came, when the tip of his tongue flicked over her most sensitive place, Brianna couldn't stop the cry of pleasure that spilled from her throat. Hands shaking in a monumental effort to keep her from collapsing onto the bed, she clamped her eyes shut and held her breath for another burn of sensation.

Another flick, then several more, then Sakis opened her wider, baring her to his gaze. He muttered something in Greek before he placed the most shocking, open-mouthed kiss on her. He devoured her as if she was his favourite meal. Sensation built upon sensation until Brianna wasn't sure which move pleased her more—his teeth grazing her clitoris or his relentlessly probing tongue inside her.

All she knew was that the majestic peak that promised both exquisite torture and intense pleasure loomed closer. Fire burned behind her closed lids. Her fingers spasmed into a death grip on her sheets. With one long, merciless pull of his mouth on her clitoris, he sent her over the edge.

He gave a long, satisfied groan as he drank her

in. For endless minutes, he lapped her with his tongue until her convulsions ceased. Vaguely, she heard him leave the bed and shuck off his trousers. Limp and breathless, she started to sag.

One hand caught her around the waist. 'Stay right there; I'm not finished with you yet.'

Brianna clawed back reason enough to demand huskily, 'Um…condom?'

'Taken care of.' His hand caressed up her stomach to cup one breast before teasing her nipple. She felt the other fumble for the loose knot in her hair. 'You know I've never seen your hair down?'

'Hmm…yes.'

He pulled her up and released the knot, then groaned as his fingers weaved through the heavy blonde tresses that went all the way down her back. '*Theos*, it's a travesty to keep this gorgeous hair tied up day after day. You deserve punishment for that, Moneypenny.'

The sharp tap on her rump sent excitement sizzling along her nerves. She bit her lip when she felt the thick evidence of his desire lying between the crease of her bottom, a relentless reminder that there was another experience to be celebrated.

'You don't think you've tortured me enough?' she asked.

His thumbs flicked over her nipples. 'Not nearly enough, *pethi mou.* Open your legs wider.'

She obeyed because she wanted this more than she wanted her next breath. At the first probe of his erection, she held her breath. He used one hand to hold her still and fed another inch inside her.

Stars burst across her vision. 'Sa—' How could it be that she was bared to him in the most intimate of ways and yet the taste of his name on her lips felt a touch too far?

'Say it,' he commanded.

'I can't…'

He started to withdraw. Her body clenched in fierce denial. 'No!'

'Say my name, Brianna.'

'Sa…Sakis,' she gasped. He pushed back in with a deep groan. 'Oh God.'

*'Again!'*

'S…Sakis!'

'Good girl.' He plunged in until he was fully embedded, then held still. 'Now, tell me how you want this to go. Fast or slow. Either way will be torture for me but I want to please you.'

Brianna wanted to tell him he'd already pleased her, a thousand times more than she'd ever imagined possible.

'Now, *glikia mou,* while my brain still functions…' Pushing her forward, he covered her with his body and trapped her splayed hands under his on the bed.

The first signs of her climax clawed at her. 'Fast, Sakis. I want it fast. And hard.'

*'Theos!'* His response through clenched teeth was a hot breath in her ear. 'Your wish is my command.' With a loud groan, he pulled out and surged back in, then proceeded to set a blistering pace that made her die a little each time her orgasm drew closer.

When he rocked back on his knees, Brianna's chest collapsed onto the bed, her feeble arms unable to sustain the barrage of sensations that rippled through her. Taking one last, gasping breath, she screamed as blissful convulsions seized her. Dimly, she heard Sakis's long, drawn-out growl as his pleasure overtook him. Deep within her, she felt his thickness pump his pleasure over and over until he was spent.

He collapsed sideways onto the bed and took her with him. In the dark room, he tucked her back against his chest, their harsh breaths gradually slowing until only the occasional spasm raked through them.

## CHAPTER EIGHT

WHAT FELT LIKE hours later, Sakis pulled her closer and brushed back her hair from her face.

The kiss he planted on her temple was gentle but possessive. 'That was sensational, *glikia mou*.'

'What does that mean?'

He gave a low laugh. 'You have an intelligent mind, Moneypenny. Find out.'

'You like to say my surname quite a lot. In fact, you don't go more than a minute or two when we're talking before going "Moneypenny this" or "Moneypenny that".'

She felt his grin against her neck. 'And this surprises you? I find your surname very intriguing, sexy.'

She fought not to tense at the interest in his tone and responded with forced lightness. 'Sexy?'

He shrugged. 'Before I met you, I'd only ever heard that name in a spy movie.'

'And you think she's sexy?'

'Extremely, and also hugely underestimated.'

'I agree with you there. But she was often overlooked in favour of sexier, in-your-face female leads; she was also the one who never got her guy.'

Sakis drew closer and traced his lips along the line of her shoulder. 'Well, I think we've remedied that tonight. Plus, she had astonishing staying power. Just like you. No one in their right mind would overlook you, Moneypenny, even though you try to hide it with that hypnotic swan-glide.'

She laughed. 'Swan glide?'

'Outwardly, you're serene, so damned efficient, and yet below you're paddling madly. Watching you juggle virtual balls is damned sexy.'

'Damn; and there I thought no one could see the mad paddling underneath.'

'Sometimes, there's just a little ruffle. Like when I misbehave and you itch to put me in my place.'

'So you know you're misbehaving? Acceptance is the first step, I suppose.'

She shivered as he rocked his hips forward in a blatantly masculine move that had her moaning. But then he pulled out of her a second later and flipped her to face him. 'Like all men in my position, I live to push the boundaries. But I get that I need an anchor sometimes. You're my anchor, Brianna.' He spoke with a low but fierce intensity that made tears prickle behind her eyes.

'Sakis...I...'

He kissed her, a slow, luxurious exploration that soon became something else, something more. She wanted to protest when he lifted his head. 'Hold that thought; I need to change condoms. Bathroom?'

She pointed and watched him head towards her tiny bathroom, her eyes glued to his toned, chiselled physique. The thought that she was about to make love with this virile, sexy man again made her tremble so hard, she clutched the pillow.

But, alone, dread began to creep in. She'd gone beyond *what the hell am I doing?* Now she had to deal with *what the hell am I going to do?*

Sakis might not have meant to but tonight he'd revealed just how much he treasured and respected her. How ironic that, just when she could've felt secure in the knowledge that her job was safe, that she didn't need to prove herself as the invaluable asset in Sakis's life, she would have to walk away.

Because there really was no choice. She would never betray Sakis the way he'd been betrayed before. As for Greg, he deserved to burn in hell.

She toyed with confessing but brushed it away. Now she understood just what he'd been through with his father, she couldn't bear for him to look at her and see another fraud, someone who'd failed to reveal the whole truth about her past.

Her only option would be to resign and find herself another job somewhere far away, perhaps in another country even, where neither Greg's vile threats or Sakis's condemnation would touch her.

A deep pool of sadness welled up inside her, bringing with it a sharp pain that made her groan and bury her face in the pillow.

She jumped when a warm hand caressed her back.

'Should I be offended that you were so far away you'd forgotten I exist?'

Composing herself, she turned to face him. *God, he was gorgeous*, even with the shadows of the past few days' stress lurking in his eyes. Perhaps that was what made him even more breathtaking—the fact that, despite being the ruthless entrepreneur feared by most competitors, he still had a caring heart.

Unable to stop herself, she reached for him and glided her hand over his warm, sculpted chest to draw him closer. 'I hadn't forgotten. I always know when you're near, Sakis. Always.'

His eyes darkened as he stretched out beside her and took her mouth in a long, deep kiss. 'I can't believe I waited this long to make you mine.'

The stamp of possessiveness in his voice made her heart jump in thrilling delight even though deep down she knew it was a futile reaction. She would never be truly his because this wouldn't last beyond the week. She pushed the disturbing thoughts away.

'Even though I was sweet enough, but nothing to lose your head over?' She quoted his words back at him and watched a shamefaced look cross his features.

He cursed under his breath. 'I think we both know that was a blatant lie.'

'What was the truth then?'

His lips drifted lazily over hers but she wasn't fooled that it was a casual caress. Against her thigh his re-energised erection pulsed with urgent demand, eliciting an electrifying reaction inside her body.

'The truth was that I wanted nothing more than to throw you on the nearest gym mat and take you until you couldn't speak. What would you have done if I'd said that, instead of the lame excuse I came up with?'

She leaned up and caught his earlobe in a saucy bite. 'I'd have said *bring it on*.'

The tremor that went through him preceded a

guttural curse as he surged over her and proceeded to claim her in the most elemental way possible.

Within seconds, he had her on the knife-edge of need, a need so visceral she didn't know whether to beg for mercy or to beg him never to stop.

'S…Sakis…please,' she begged as he roughly tongued one nipple.

'I love the sound of my name on your lips. Say it again,' he murmured against her skin, his gaze rising to capture hers.

She shook her head in silent denial. A fiercely determined light entered his eyes and her heart sank.

He tugged on her engorged nub. 'Say my name, Brianna.'

'Why?' she asked defiantly.

'Because there's something potent and infinitely sexy about you crying out my name in the heat of passion.'

'But it sounds… It feels…'

'Too intimate?' He continued the erotic path between her breasts, his gaze never leaving hers as she nodded. 'It makes it all the more intense, no?'

Firm hands parted her thighs and one thumb lazily stroked her.

'Yes.' She sucked in a jagged breath as arousal spiked her blood with drugging pleasure. Her lids grew heavy and her back arched off the bed as the pressure escalated.

'That's it; lose yourself in it, Brianna…'

The lazy, continental drawl of her name had the right effect. Liquid heat oozed through her, making her limbs grow heavy and weak. *'Oh God.'*

'Wrong deity,' he said on a low laugh. The sound grazed over her, adding another dimension to the emotions bombarding her. Teeth bit her inner thigh; his warm tongue immediately soothed the bite, then proceeded to draw in ever closer circles to where his thumb wrecked mindless chaos.

Pleasure roared through her, eliciting the exact response she knew he wanted.

*Sakis.* The name echoed through her, over and over, seeking release. *Sakis.*

Her skin tightened as her climax grew closer. His tongue lapped her once, twice.

At the outer reaches of her mind, she heard a tearing sound.

Sakis.

His thumb left her clitoris and was replaced immediately by his tongue. Brianna shut her eyes on a long, keening moan that was ripped from the depths of her soul.

Dear Lord, she was going to come like she never

had before. She reached out, intending to grip the sheets, and instead encountered hot, muscled flesh.

Her eyes flew open just as he reared above her and plunged, hot, stiff and deep inside her.

'Sakis!'

'Yes! *Theos*, you look so hot like that.'

She repeated his name in a strangled litany as the most forceful orgasm she'd ever had laid her to waste. Through it all he kept up the rhythm, his groans of pleasure prolonging hers, so she milked him with her muscles.

'Brianna, *eros mou*.' He fell onto his elbows and plunged his fingers into her hair, holding her down as he plundered her mouth with his. 'You're incredible,' he breathed against her lips as he surged deeper inside her. 'I can't get enough of you.'

His fingers tightened in her hair as his mouth drifted over her jaw to her neck. His breath grew harsh, his body momentarily losing its steady rhythm as waves of pleasure washed over them.

Gritting his teeth, Sakis forced back control into his body, if only temporarily, because he knew he was fighting a losing battle. But it was a battle he was perfectly willing to surrender.

The warm, sexy body undulating beneath him blew his mind. While half of him declared himself insane for waiting this long to give in to the spellbinding attraction, the other half rejoiced at waiting. It was clear Brianna wouldn't have given in under normal circumstances.

Something had happened today at the café. He didn't know what and couldn't pinpoint it but the simple meal had taken an unexpected turn, had shaken him in a way that had left him reeling.

She'd felt it too; he knew it. Whether it was the reason she'd ended up here, he didn't know, but he intended to grasp this golden opportunity with both hands.

Her inner muscles tightened again and he nearly lost it. The swollen temptation of her roughly kissed mouth parted on a breath and he groaned. Sweet heaven, everything about her blew his mind, but never in a thousand years had he dreamed the sex with her would be this great, this intense.

She breathed his name again, as if now she'd given herself permission to use it she couldn't say it enough. That was okay with him…more than okay. The sound of his name on her lips was a potent aphrodisiac all by itself.

He was leaning down to take those impossibly delectable lips again when he saw it. Buried beneath the cascade of her hair was an elegant scroll across her left collarbone.

She surged blindly up at that moment, impatient for his kiss, and her hair fell away.

'I refuse to sink', the tattoo read. And beside it was a tiny etching of a soaring phoenix.

He already knew she was brave beyond words. The glimpse of her life she'd shared with him had alerted him to a not-so-rosy past, perhaps a harsh childhood. Sakis was struck again by how little he really knew of her. Nevertheless, he knew he didn't need to dig to find out she had a core of integrity that had remained unblemished, despite whatever adversities she'd faced.

The knowledge jolted something deep and alien inside him. Shockingly, he desired her even more. He bucked into her and revelled in her hitched breathing. But he wanted more; felt an unrelenting need to touch her in the way she'd touched him tonight.

'Open your eyes, *pethi mou*,' he demanded hoarsely.

Slowly her lids parted, displaying exquisite turquoise eyes drenched in desire. 'What?'

'I want you to see me, Brianna. Feel what you do to me and know that I appreciate you more than you know.'

Her mouth dropped open in wordless wonder. Unable to help himself, he kissed her again. Then all too soon the climax that had been building inexorably surged with brutal force. He spread her thighs wider and pumped hard and fast inside her.

Her cry of ecstasy echoed his own minutes later as he came in a torrent of dizzying pleasure.

He waited until their breaths had returned to normal before he brushed aside her hair and looked closely at the tattoo. Slowly, he let his finger drift over it, telling himself he'd imagined it, when she stiffened.

'This is interesting…'

The invitation to confess was blatant.

But Brianna couldn't open that can of worms. Not after she'd already opened so much of herself that she was sure Sakis could see straight through her by now. God, how had she imagined that she could just live in this moment, satisfy the clawing need then walk away?

With just a handful of words, Sakis had split her heart wide open.

*I want you to see me... You're my anchor, Brianna... I appreciate you more than you know.*

'Brianna?' The demand was more powerful.

She scrambled to find a reasonable explanation. 'I got it after I left my…my last job…' She stopped, her heart hammering as she realised that she was highly emotional from their love-making and really shouldn't be talking.

'Most people take a holiday between jobs. But you got a tattoo?' Scarily, his curiosity had deepened. 'And a symbolic one, at that. Did you feel as if you were sinking?' His fingers drifted over the words again, and despite her roiling emotions she shivered with fresh need.

She forced a laugh. 'I guess I'm not most people.' *Stop talking now. Stop. Stop. Stop!* 'And yes, I felt like I was sinking. For a while I lost my way.' God, no…

His fingers touched the phoenix then he brushed it with his mouth. 'But then you triumphed.'

She let out a shaky breath. 'Y-yes.'

'Hmm, we're agreed on one thing—you're not most people. You're exquisitely unique.' His hand drifted down, paused over her breast then trailed lower to touch the scar on her hip. 'And this?'

Her breath caught anew. How had she thought he wouldn't notice? He'd spent an inordinate amount of time exploring every inch of her body, much to her shameless delight. Of course Sakis's astute gaze would've caught the slightly puckered flesh where the sharp, white-hot lance of the inmate's blade had stabbed deep and ruptured her spleen.

'I…I was attacked. It was a mugging.' That at least was the truth. What she couldn't confess was where she'd been when it had happened.

His fingers stilled then he swore hard. 'When?'

'Two years ago.'

He cupped her jaw. 'Was your attacker caught?'

Brianna shut her eyes against the probing of his. 'Yes, they were caught. And there was even some semblance of justice.' If you could call six months' solitary confinement for a prisoner already serving life 'justice'.

That seemed to satisfy Sakis. When she risked a glance at him, the harshness she'd heard in his voice was not evident in his face. 'Good,' he breathed as his fingers resumed its bone-melting caress. 'I'm glad.'

Before she could draw another breath, his head dropped and his lips touched the puckered scar. Her skin heated then burned as his lips, then his tongue moved over her flesh.

She expected him to ask about her ankle tattoo, the one she'd caught him eyeing on the plane. But he seemed to have regained his zealous exploration of her body.

Her breath hitched as his mouth wreaked blissful havoc. Within seconds, her brain ceased to function.

* * *

Brianna woke to the sound of movement in her bedroom. Struggling up from an exquisitely saucy dream featuring Sakis, she opened her eyes to find him standing at the foot of her bed, his gaze on her as he secured his cufflinks.

The look on his face immediately gripped her attention. Gone was the lover who'd whispered ardent words of pleasure and worship against her skin last night. In its place was Sakis, billionaire shipping magnate. But, as she watched, she saw the mask slip to reveal the stress he hadn't completely banished.

'I have to go,' he said. 'There's been a development.'

Brianna sat up and pushed her hair from her face. 'What?'

His fingers stilled on his cuff. 'The bodies of two crew-members have been found.'

Shock and grief rocked through her in equal measures. 'When did you find out?'

'Ten minutes ago. They were found two miles away where converging tides had hidden the bodies. The investigators think they drowned.'

She started to throw the covers off, experienced a fierce wave of self-consciousness and talked herself out of it. This wasn't the time. 'Give me ten minutes to shower and I'll come with you. I… We need to see about getting them home.'

He rounded the bed and stopped in front of her. One hand caressed her cheek. 'It's been taken care of. I woke my head of HR. Those men died on my company's watch so they're my responsibility. He's arranging everything, but I'm meeting the families this morning to express my condolences…' He stopped and breathed in deep.

A wave of sadness washed over her. 'It wasn't the outcome any of us wanted. Which two were found?'

'The deputy captain and the first officer.'

'So there's still no sign of Morgan Lowell?'

'No.'

Which meant they still had no answer to what had happened to the tanker. 'I'll do my best to keep it out of the press but there are no guarantees.' She strove for a semblance of professionalism—professionalism which became precarious as his arms banded around her waist and pulled her closer. Desire's inferno raged through her body.

'It's all been handled. Foyle assures me there's a procedure to dealing with this. We can't do anything more.'

'So for now I'm redundant?'

'Never,' he breathed. 'You will never be redundant to me.'

The intensity of his answer sent alarm skittering over her skin. She was in danger of fooling herself again. In danger of believing that Sakis was beginning to want her, to need her the way she'd once dreamed of being needed.

Forcing a laugh, she pulled out of his arms. 'Never say never. Shower time; I'll be out in ten.' She backed away, all the while noting he remained where he stood, his intense eyes on her. 'Um, there's coffee in the kitchen if you want some. I'm afraid I don't have much in the way of food as I wasn't expecting to stop here last night.'

Finally, he nodded. 'Coffee will suffice.'

Brianna held her breath until he left her room, then flew into the bathroom.

Eight minutes later she was slipping on high-heeled designer leopard-print shoes as she pinned her hair up in its usual chignon. With one last look to check her appearance, she tugged the sleeves of her black Prada suit, picked up her large handbag containing her tablet and left the room.

Sakis stood at her tiny living-room window gazing down at the street below. He turned at her entrance and handed her the second cup in his hand just before his phone buzzed. As she sipped her coffee, Brianna couldn't stop staring at the magnificent man who paced her living room.

A man who'd not only taken her body but had found his way into parts of her heart she'd imagined had withered and died.

The thought of walking away from this man for ever gouged her with pain that left her breathless. When he speared her with those mesmerising eyes, she fought hard to stop her feelings from showing.

She would have time to deal with the heartache later. Because, of course, there would be heartache. Her feelings for Sakis had gone way beyond the professional. She'd known that before she'd slept with him last night. This morning, watching him struggle with fresh adversity made those feelings more intense.

So intense she set her coffee cup down before her trembling hands gave her away. 'Do you need anything else before we leave?'

'Yes. Come here.'

She went willingly, unable to resist him. He looked around the room then set the coffee mug on the window sill. 'You'll enlighten me as to why this apartment has barely any furniture in it later, but for now I have a greater need.'

'What?'

He pulled her closer and cupped her face in his

large hands. 'I haven't said good morning properly. I may not get the chance once we leave here.' He sealed his mouth over hers in a long, exploratory kiss. When he finally lifted his head, his eyes were the dark green she associated with extreme emotion. 'Good morning, *pethi mou*,' he murmured.

'G-good morning,' she responded in a voice husky with fresh need.

Reluctantly he dropped his hand and stepped back. 'Let's get out of here now or we'll never leave.'

The journey to the office was completed in near silence. Sakis seemed lost in thought, his answers monosyllabic as she tried to slip back into professional mode.

As they entered the underground car park at Pantelides Towers, she couldn't bear it any more. Turning to him, she waited until he faced her. 'If you're wondering how to play this, you need not worry. No one needs to know about what happened last night. I know what happened with Giselle—'

'Is ancient history. What's going on between us is different.'

Her heart lurched then hammered. 'You mean you don't mind if anyone finds out?'

He stiffened. 'I didn't say that.'

The hurt that scythed through her was as unbearable as it was irrational.

When the car stopped she scrambled to get out. Sakis grabbed her arm to stay her and waved the driver away when he approached.

'Wait, that didn't come out right. What I meant was that the last thing I want is for you to be caught in the crosshairs because of my past. It's very easy for the wrong person to put two and two together and come up with fifteen. You don't deserve to suffer for my father's sins.'

She sagged backwards. 'Was he… He wasn't always that bad, was he?' It was unthinkable that they both could've suffered such outwardly different, but inwardly similar and painful upbringings. At least, she hoped not, because her heart ached for the pain in his voice every time he spoke about his father.

She had come to terms, somewhat, with her non-relationship with her mother.

He sucked in a long breath. 'Yes, he was. He was a philanderer and an extortionist who was corrupt to the core and very clever at hiding his true colours. When his deeds were finally uncovered, our lives were turned inside out. Our every word and deed was scrutinised. Several times, our house staff discovered tabloid journalists digging through our garbage in the middle of the night, looking for more dirt.'

Distress for him scythed through her. 'That's horrible.'

'As horrible as that was, I mistakenly thought that was the worst of it.'

She was almost afraid to ask. 'What else did you find?'

'It turned out my father had mistresses stashed all over the globe, not just the secretary who'd grown tired of his philandering ways and empty promises—she was the one who blew the whistle that started the ball rolling, by the way. Once the first mistress crawled out of the woodwork, they were unstoppable. And you know why they all came forward, every single one of them?'

She shook her head despite the dread crawling through her stomach.

'*Money.* With my father's arrest and all our assets frozen, they knew the money that funded their lavish lifestyles would dry up. They had to sell their stories quickly and to the highest bidder before they became yesterday's news—regardless of the fact that their actions would push my mother into attempting to take her own life.'

She gasped. '*God*, I'm so sorry, Sakis.'

Pain was etched deep on his face but he slid his

fingers through hers and brought her hand up to his mouth. But, although his touch was gentle, the gleam in his was anything but. 'So you see why I find it hard to trust the motives of others?'

Dry-mouthed, she nodded. 'I do, but it doesn't hurt to occasionally give the benefit of the doubt.' The knowledge that she was silently pleading for herself sent a wave of shame through her.

His gaze raked her face, his own features a harsh stamp of implacability. Then slowly, as she watched, his face relaxed. He reached across and cupped her face, pulled her close and kissed her.

'For you, Brianna, I'm willing to suspend my penchant for expecting the worst, to let go of my bias and cynicism—because, believe me, in this instance I relish the chance to be proved wrong.'

But he wasn't proved wrong.

At three o'clock that afternoon, Richard Moorecroft rang with a full confession for his part in the tanker crash.

# CHAPTER NINE

AN HOUR LATER, Sakis was pacing his office when he heard his head of security enter and exchange greetings with Brianna.

'Get in here, both of you!' he bellowed, the anger he was fighting to contain roiling just beneath his skin.

He turned from his desk as they entered. He tried to concentrate on his security chief. But, as if it acted independent of his control, his gaze strayed to Brianna.

She was as contained and self-assured as he'd always known her to be. There was no trace of the woman who'd writhed beneath him last night, screaming her pleasure as he'd taken her to the heights of ecstasy, or the gentle soul who'd listened to him spill his guts about his father in the car, her eyes haunted with pain for him.

He wanted to hate her for her poise and calm but he realised that he admired her for it—something *else* he admired about her. *Theos*, his list of things he admired about Brianna Moneypenny grew by the day. Anyone would think she meant more to him than—

His mind screeched to a halt but his legs were weakening with the force of the unknown emotion that smashed through him. Folding his arms, he gritted his teeth and perched on the edge of his desk.

'What do you have for me?' he demanded from Sheldon.

'As you requested, we dug a little deeper into the financials of First Mate Isaacs and Deputy Captain Green. A deposit of one hundred thousand euros was made into each of their accounts seven days ago.'

Sakis's hands tightened around his biceps as bitterness tightened like a vice around his chest. 'Have we traced the source of the funds?' Even now when he had the evidence, he didn't want to believe his employees were guilty.

Only this morning, he would've believed the worst. But Brianna's caution to give them the benefit of the doubt had settled deep within him. When he'd given her words further thought he'd realised how much he'd let cynicism rule his life. Letting go even a little had felt...liberating. He'd breathed easier for the first time in a very long time.

But now the hard ache was back full force along with memories he couldn't seem to bury easily.

'Moorecroft used about half a dozen shell companies to obfuscate his activities. Without his confession it'd have taken a few more days but knowing where to look helped. It also helped that the crew members did nothing to hide the money they received,' Sheldon said.

'Because they thought they were home free,' Sakis rasped. The confirmation from Moorecroft that he'd paid his crew to deliberately crash his tanker to spark a hostile takeover made a tide of rage rise within him. Sakis could forgive the damage to his vessel—it was insured and he would be more than compensated for it once the investigation was over. But it was the senseless loss of lives he couldn't stomach, along with the fact that the rest of his crew had been put at severe risk.

After his phone call with Moorecroft, with the pain-racked faces of his dead employees' families fresh in his mind, he hadn't hesitated to let his broken adversary know to expect full criminal charges against him.

He'd experienced a twinge when he'd looked up from the phone call and caught Brianna's expression but he'd pushed the feeling away.

Greed had driven another man to put others' lives at risk. There was no way he could forgive that.

'What about Lowell's account?'

'We're trying to access it but it's a bit more complicated.'

Sakis frowned. 'How complicated?'

'His salary was wired to a routing account that went to a Swiss bank account. Those are a little tougher to crack.'

Surprise shot him upright. He turned to Brianna. 'Did we flag that up in his HR details?'

She bit her lip. Heat flared in his groin, followed closely by another guilty twinge for his harsh tone. 'No,' she answered.

Sakis sucked in a deep breath. 'That will be all, Sheldon. Let me know as soon as you have anything new.'

Sheldon nodded and left.

Silence reigned for several minutes. Then Brianna walked forward. 'I'm expecting an "I told you so".'

He settled his attention fully on her in a way he'd been reluctant to do with another person in the room. Even now he feared his features would betray the extent of the alien emotions roaring through him.

*Theos*, he needed a drink. *Why the hell not?*

'There's no point. It is what it is.'

'Then why are you pouring yourself a drink in the middle of a work day?'

'It's not the middle of the day, it's almost five o'clock.'

'It's five o'clock for most people but for you it's not, since you work till midnight most nights.'

Sakis barely glanced at the fifty-year-old single malt as he lifted it to his lips and drained it. 'If you must know, I'm trying to understand what drives anyone to depths of betrayal such as this with little regard for how it'll hurt their family and people who care about them.'

She started to come towards him and his senses leapt, but at the last moment she veered away and started straightening the papers on his desk. Sakis barely stopped himself from growling his frustration.

'And are you getting any answers from the bottom of your glass?'

He slammed the glass down and strode to where she stood. 'Are you trying to rile me? Because, trust me, you're succeeding.'

'I'm just trying to make you see that you can't blame yourself for the choices other people make. You can either forgive them or…'

'Or?'

For a single moment, her face creased with something similar to the bitterness and despair clawing through him. 'Or you can cut them out of your life, I suppose.'

He frowned. 'Who cut you out of their life, Brianna?'

Stark pain washed over her features before she tried to mask it. 'This isn't about me.'

He took her by the arms. 'It most definitely is. What did she do to you?'

She made a sound that caught and tightened around his heart. The sort of sound a wounded animal made when they were frightened.

'She…she chose drugs over me.' She stopped and sucked in a gulping breath. 'I don't really want to talk about this.'

'You encouraged me to bare my soul to you this morning. I think it's only fair that you do the same.'

'More therapy?' She tried pull away but he held fast.

'Tell me about her. Where is she? Is she still alive?'

A sad little shiver went through her. 'Yes, she's alive. But we're not in touch. We haven't been for a while.'

'Why not?'

She cast a desperate glance around, anywhere

but at him. 'Sakis, this isn't right. I'm your… You're my boss.'

'We went way beyond that last night. Answer my question, unless you wish me to demonstrate our revised positions?'

Her lips parted on a tiny gasp that made him want to plunge his tongue between them but he restrained himself. For once, the need to see beneath the surface of Brianna Moneypenny trumped everything else.

'I…I've already told you I didn't grow up in the best of circumstances. Because of her drug habit we…lived on the street from when I was about four until I was ten. Sometimes I went for days without a proper meal.'

Shock slammed through Sakis. For several moments he was unable to reconcile the woman who stood before him, poised and breathtakingly stunning, with the bedraggled, haunted image she portrayed.

'How… Why?' he demanded, cursing silently when he saw her pale face.

Bruised eyes finally met his. 'She couldn't hold down a job for longer than a couple of weeks but she was cunning enough to evade the authorities for the better part of six years. But finally her luck—if you can call it that—ran out. Social Services took me away from her when I was ten. I found her when I turned eighteen.'

Another bolt of shock went through him. 'You *found* her? After what she did to you, you went to look for her?'

Her eyes darkened with pain. When his hands slid down her arms to hers, she gripped him tight. But he knew her mind was firmly in the past.

'She was my mother. Don't get me wrong, I hated her for a long time, but I had to eventually accept the fact that she was also a human being caught in the grip of an addiction that almost ruined her life,' she said.

Sakis saw her raw pain, clenched his jaw and silently cursed the woman who'd done this to her. More than anything, he wanted to obliterate her pain.

*Theos, what the hell was happening to him?*

*Wait...* 'Almost?'

She gave a jerky nod. 'She got it together in the end. In the eight years we were apart, she beat her addiction and got her act together. I...can't help but think I was the one who was holding her back.'

His growled curse made her jump. Leaning down, he kissed her hard and fast.

'She never made an effort to kick her habit when I

was around. And she would get this look in her eyes whenever she looked at me—like she hated me.'

Sakis wanted to swear again, but he bit his tongue. 'No child should ever be blamed for being born. She had a duty to look after you. She failed. So she got herself better, then what?'

'She remarried and had another child.'

'So, it was a happy ending for her?' He couldn't stop a hint of bitterness from spilling out. He and his brothers hadn't been granted a happy ending. And his mother continued to live a hollow existence, a shadow of the vibrant woman she'd been for the first decade of his life. 'But she cut you from her life?'

'Yes; I suppose she didn't want the reminder,' she answered lightly; a little too breezily.

Sakis knew she was glossing over her pain. Wasn't it the same way he'd glossed over his for years? But something else struck him, made him reel all over again.

She'd had a mother who had done her wrong in the most fundamental of ways—she'd failed to look after her daughter when she was young and helpless and needed her most. And yet, Brianna had gone out of her way to find her after she was grown and on her own two feet.

The depth of compassion behind such forgiveness rocked him to his soul. 'I never forgave my father for what he did to us, and especially what he did to my mother. Hell, sometimes I think he purposefully died of a heart attack in her arms just to twist the knife in further, because she sure as hell almost died mourning him.'

She touched his cheek with fingers that trembled. 'Don't be too hard on her. She had her heart broken the same way yours was.'

But then he'd had his brothers and the myriad cousins, aunts and uncles who'd rallied round when the going had got tough. Even in his darkest days, there'd always been someone around and, although he'd never been one to reach out, deep down he'd known there was someone around.

*Whereas, Brianna had had nobody.*

His insides clenched with the same emotion he'd experienced earlier. Like a magnet drawn to her irresistible presence, he pulled her closer.

'You're amazing, do you know that?' he murmured against her hair, satisfied for the moment to just hold her close like this.

'I am?' Her delicate eyelids fluttered as she looked up at him.

'Yes. You have a unique way of holding up a mirror to some of my deeply held beliefs that make me question them.'

She gave a shaky laugh. 'And that's a good thing?'

'Forcing me to examine them is a good thing. Learning to forgive is another…' He felt her stiffen but she felt too good in his arms for him to question her reaction. 'But perhaps I can try to understand the reason why people act the way they do.'

When she tried to pull away, he reluctantly let her place several inches between them.

'I should get back to work.'

Sakis frowned. He didn't want distance. He didn't like the threat of tears in her eyes. But already he could feel her withdrawing.

Belatedly, he remembered where they were.

But so what? They were alone in his inner sanctum. No one would dare breach it without incurring his wrath. Besides, both his door and hers were shut. And all he wanted was a quick kiss. Well…he gave an inner grimace…he wanted way more than that but…

He focused to find her halfway to the door. What the hell…?

In swift strides he reached the door and slammed his hand against the heavy polished steel-and-timber frame, the feeling that he was missing something fundamental eating away at him. She jumped, her wide-eyed gaze swinging to his.

'What's the matter?' he demanded.

'Nothing. I'm just going back to my desk, Mr—'

'Don't you even dare think about calling me that!'

'Okay.' She licked her plump lower lip. 'Sakis... can I go back to my desk?'

His ire grew along with his hard-on. He grasped her waist. 'After what just happened? No way.'

She eyed the closed door with a longing he wanted transferred to him, preferably with single-minded devotion to the granite-hard part of his anatomy. 'Please...'

He tracked back over their conversation and sighed. 'I can't change who I am overnight, Brianna. Forgiveness comes easily to you, but I'm going to need time.'

Her eyes widened even further with alarm. 'I don't want you to change...not unless you want to. I mean, I'm not invested in anything here...with you. Certainly not enough to warrant you going out of your way to make those sorts of reassurances.'

Those words spilling from her lips sent him into the stratosphere. With a snarl born of frustration, anxiety and piercing arousal, he locked the door, caught her around the waist and swung her up in his arms.

*'Sakis!'*

'Let's just see how invested you are, shall we?'

'Put me down!'

Ignoring her demand, he carried her to the desk she'd straightened so efficiently minutes ago. Setting her on the edge, he slashed one hand across the polished surface, sending the papers flying.

'I seriously hope you don't expect me to clean that up!' Her colour was hectic, her breath coming out in pants as she glared at him.

*Yes*, this was what he wanted: her fire, her spirit. He hated the sad, frightened, achingly lonely Brianna. He hated cool, calm and distant Brianna even more, especially after last night. Not after seeing the generous heart and fiery passion that resided beneath the prim exterior.

'If that's what I desire, then you shall do it, no?'

Her chin rose and his senses roared. 'In your dreams. My job description doesn't include cleaning up after you. I'm not your chambermaid.'

He caught her hands and planted them on his chest. 'As of last night, your job description includes doing whatever pleases me in the bedroom.'

Despite her protests, her fingers curled into his chest. He nearly shouted with triumph and relief. 'We're not in the bedroom. Besides, what about what I want?'

His hand fisted in her hair, sought and found

the hidden clasp and tugged. Vibrant golden hair spilled over his arm. Using it, he pulled her close until his jaw grazed her soft cheek. 'Call this mutually beneficial therapy. Besides, I'm a quick study, *glikia mou.* I know *exactly* what you want.'

Her breath caught, making him laugh. He pushed her back, using her slight imbalance to swiftly undo the single button of her jacket. It was off before she could take another surprised breath.

'Sakis, for goodness' sake! We're in your office.'

'My *locked* office. And it's the end of the day for everyone else except us.'

'I still think…'

He kissed her, the temptation too much to resist. That it effectively shut her up was a great bonus, as was her fractured moan that vibrated through him.

He made easy work of the zipper of her dress and slid it off with minimal protest. He didn't notice what she wore beneath until he spread her backwards across his desk. A strangled choke made its way up his throat as he froze.

'*Theos*, tell me you haven't been wearing lingerie like these since you started working for me?'

A provocative smile dispelled the nervous apprehension on her face. 'Fine. I won't.'

She stretched under his gaze, arching her back in a sinuous move that made him think of a sleek cat.

Over the top of the bustier bra that connected the garter to the top of her sheer stockings, the plump slopes of her breasts taunted him. His mouth watered and his fingers itched to touch with a need so strong he staggered forward. Roughly he pulled one cup down and circled a rosy nipple with his tongue.

Her ragged cry of delight was music to his ears, because the knowledge that he wasn't in this insane feeling alone soothed a stunned and confused part of him.

He rolled the nub in his mouth and tugged with his teeth while he frantically undressed. Naked, he straightened and glanced down at her, spread across his desk like a decadent offering. Struck dumb, he just stared at her stunning perfection.

'You're about to tell me you've imagined me spread out like this across your desk, aren't you?' she asked huskily.

Surprisingly, this particular scenario had never once crossed his mind. 'No, and it's a good thing too. I don't think I'd ever have got any work done if I had a picture such as this in my mind,' he rasped, his voice thick and alien. 'I've imagined you elsewhere though—in my shower, across the back seat of my car, in my lift…'

A shiver went through her. 'Your lift?'

'*Ne*. In my mind, my private lift has seen a lot of action featuring you in very many compromising ways. But *this* beats even my most fevered imaginings.'

He continued to stare at the vision before him. He must have stared for too long because she started to squirm. With one hand he held her down. With the other, he pulled down the skimpiest thong ever created and slid his hands between her thighs. Her wet heat coated his fingers and in that moment Sakis believed he'd never been so turned on. The next moment, he realised he was wrong.

Brianna laid her hand on his thigh and that simple action sent his heart rate soaring out of control. Then her hand moved upward...and her searching fingers boldly settled over his hard length.

*'Theos!'*

'Wrong deity,' she responded saucily.

His laugh scraped his throat as she gripped him hard. From root to tip, she caressed him, over and over, until he was sure he'd lost his hold on reality. His altered state was why he didn't read her intention when she moistened her lip and wriggled down his desk. Before he could admonish her for not staying put, she boldly took him in her perfect mouth.

'Brianna!' He slammed a hand on the desk to

steady himself against the deep shudder powering through him. The sight of him in her mouth nearly unmanned him. His breath hissed out as he fought not to gush his climax like a hormonal teenager right then and there. He groaned deep and long as her tongue swirled over him and her hand pumped, teased, threatened to blow his mind to smithereens. '*Yes!* Just like that!'

He suffered the sweet torture until the tell-tale tightening forced him to pull back. When she clung and made a sound of protest, Sakis seriously considered giving in, but no…

The chance to take her again, stamp his possession on her, was paramount. He needed to obliterate that distance he'd sensed her trying to put between them. The reason for it was irrelevant. The need was too strong to question.

He trailed hot kisses down her body, making her squirm anew for him. The seconds it took to locate and put on the condom felt like decades. But at last he parted her thighs and positioned himself at her entrance. She lifted her head and looked at him, her expression one of rapt hunger that almost equalled his own.

'Are you invested in this?' he rasped.

A glimmer of alarm skittered through her eyes. 'Sakis…'

'Are you? Because I am, Brianna.'

Her mouth parted on a shocked exhalation. 'Please, Sakis, don't say that.'

'Why not?'

'Because you don't mean it.'

'Yes, I do. I fought it for as long as I could, but in the end it was no use. I want you. I want this. Do you want it too?'

Her breath shivered out of her. 'Y-yes. I want this.'

He plunged into her, perhaps a little more roughly than he'd intended, but his need was too great. Watching her breasts bounce with each thrust, Sakis wondered if a heart had ever burst from too much excitement, too much need.

Because, even as he took her to the brink, he realised it wasn't enough. He'd never get enough of Brianna. But this... *Theos*, this was a brilliant start. Later he would pause to examine his feelings a little bit more, reassure himself exactly what he was dealing with and how best to handle the strange feelings inside him. Because something *was* happening to him. Something he couldn't define.

As his brain melted from pleasure overload, he let his hands drift upward in a slow caress. His fingers grazed her scar and a feeling of primitive rage rose through him at the person who'd done this to her. If he hadn't received Brianna's reassurance that justice had been done, he'd have hunted the culprit down and torn him apart with his bare hands.

Overwhelming protectiveness—another alien feeling he had to grapple with. Gripping her nape, he forced her up to receive his kiss as he surged one last time inside her, felt her spasm around him and let go.

The rush was the best yet. With a groan that stemmed from his soul, he shut his eyes and gave in to it. It was a long time before reality descended on him again.

Brianna's arms tightened around Sakis as their breaths returned to normal, fear clutching her heart.

She'd spilled her guts to him about her mother. He'd been outraged on her behalf. He'd shown her sympathy that had touched her soul and made her realise that, while she'd forgiven her mother for an addiction she hadn't been able to conquer, it was the pain of her abandonment when she was clean that hurt the most.

But Sakis had readily admitted forgiveness was a rare commodity to *him*.

She tried to tell herself it didn't matter. Come Friday, when her time ran out, she would be out of here. Greg had taken to sending her hourly reminders of her deadline. To stop Sakis from getting suspicious, she'd put her phone on silent and zipped it out of sight in her jacket pocket.

But her imminent departure wasn't the reason she'd given Sakis a glimpse into her past.

It was because she'd desperately wanted him to see her—not the ruthlessly efficient personal assistant but *her*, Brianna Moneypenny, the person who'd started life as Anna Simpson, daughter of a crackhead, and then had taken her grandmother's maiden name and forged a new identity for herself.

She'd bared herself to Sakis, and now she felt more vulnerable than ever.

His stance on betrayal remained rigid. If he ever found out about her past, he would never forgive her for bringing her soiled reputation to his company.

'I can hear you thinking,' he said, his voice a husky muffle against her neck.

'I've just had sex with you on your desk. That merits a little bit of thinking time, don't you think?'

'Perhaps. But, since it's going to be a familiar feature in our relationship, I suggest you get used to it.'

He heard her sudden intake of breath. Rearing up, he rested on his elbows and speared her with a probing look. One she couldn't meet for long before she settled her gaze on the pulse beating in his neck. 'The word "relationship" frightens you?'

She willed her pulse to slow, forcing the hope that had no business fluttering in her chest to die a swift death. There could be no future between them. None.

'Not the word, no, but I think this is going a little too…fast. We only started sleeping together last night.'

'After eighteen months of holding back. I think asking for restraint right now is asking for the impossible. I'll need several weeks at least to take the edge off.'

She looked into intense green eyes. 'You warned me at my interview, conducted across this very desk, not to even dream of getting involved with you.'

He had the grace to look shamefaced, but even that look held a lethal charm that doomed her. 'It was so soon after Giselle; I was still angry. Everyone I'd interviewed reminded me of her. You were the first one who didn't. When I found myself getting attracted to you, I fought it with everything I had because I didn't want that nasty business repeating itself.'

Unable to resist, she slid her fingers through his thick hair. 'She really did a number on you, didn't she?'

His smile was wry. 'I'm not beyond admitting I was blinded to her true nature until it was much too late.'

'Wow, I'm not sure whether to be pleased or disappointed that you're fallible.'

He straightened and picked her up from his desk as if she weighed nothing. 'I never claimed to be perfect, except when it comes to winning rowing championships. Then I'm unequalled,' he boasted as he started to stride across the office.

'Modesty is such a rare and beautiful thing, Sakis.'

His deep, unfettered laugh made her heart swell with pleasure. 'Yes, so is the ability to state things as they are.'

'No one will accuse you of being a wallflower. Wait, where are you taking me?'

'Upstairs, to get you therapeutically wet and soapy in my shower.'

'I think you're taking this therapy thing a bit far. Sakis, put me down. Our clothes!' She wriggled until he let her slide down his body to stand upright.

'Leave them.' He keyed in the code for his turbo lift.

'Absolutely not. No way am I letting the cleaner find my knickers and stuff all over your office floor!' She ran back and started gathering them. 'And don't just stand there, pick up your own damn clothes.'

With a husky laugh, Sakis followed and picked up his discarded clothes. Then, because she really couldn't stand to leave them, she gathered the strewn papers and placed them back on the desk. When his mocking laugh deepened, she rounded on him.

'Next time, you pick them up yourself.'

He caught her to him and smacked her lightly on the bottom. When she yelped, he kissed her. 'That's for disobeying me again. But I like that you admit there'll be a next time.'

She looked up and her gaze caught his. For the first time, she glimpsed a vulnerability she'd never seen before in his eyes. As if he hadn't been sure she would let anything like what had happened occur between them again.

Desolation caught at her heart. She would pay a steep price for letting this thing continue but the need to be with him in every way until she left was too strong. Going closer, she raised herself on tiptoe and kissed along his jaw.

'There'll be a next time only if I get to go on top.'

Sakis jerked awake to the sound of a phone buzzing. Beside him Brianna was out cold, worn out from the relentless demands he'd made of her body. The same lethargy swirled through him, making him toy with the idea of ignoring the phone.

The buzzing increased.

Rubbing the sleep from his eyes, he started to reach for his phone, but realised the ringing was from Brianna's.

Getting off the bed, he hunted through their discarded clothes until he located the phone in her jacket pocket.

Palming it, Sakis hesitated again. Relief coursed through him when it stopped ringing. But, almost immediately, it started to buzz again. With an impatient sigh, he pressed the button.

'Anna?' A man's impatient voice, one he didn't recognise. Not that he had first-hand knowledge of the men who called Brianna, of course… A spike of intense dislike filled him at the thought of anyone who'd been given the permission to call her…*Anna*?

Sakis frowned. 'You've got the wrong number. This is *Brianna's* phone. Who is this?'

*And why the hell are you calling at three a.m.?*

Silence greeted his demand. A moment later, the line went dead.

Sakis pulled the phone away and searched for the number. It was blocked.

Dropping her jacket, he went back to bed and set the phone down on the bedside table. He tucked his arms beneath his head, unable to stem the unease that spiralled through his gut.

He had no grounds to suspect anything other than a wrongly dialled number. It could be pure coincidence that another man had called his lover demanding to speak to *Anna.*

And yet, Sakis was still awake two hours later, unable to shake the mild dread. When the phone pinged with an incoming message, he snatched it up before it could wake her.

With a sinking feeling in the pit of his stomach, he slid his thumb across the interactive surface. Again the number was blocked but the words on the screen iced his spine:

*Just a friendly reminder that you have three days to get me what I need. G.*

# CHAPTER TEN

*IT'S NOTHING. YOU'RE blowing things out of proportion.*

Sakis repeated the words over and over as he pulled the handles of the rowing machine in his gym just after six o'clock. Right this moment he'd have loved to be doing the real thing but this wasn't the time to jump in his car and drive to his rowing club, no matter how powerful the temptation.

He smothered the voice that suggested he was running away from the truth.

*What truth?*

He didn't know what the text on Brianna's phone meant. Sure, the easiest thing would've been to wake her up and demand an answer. Instead, he'd got up, returned the phone to her jacket pocket and high-tailed it to the gym.

He yanked on the row bars and welcomed the burn of pain between his shoulders and the sweat that poured off his skin. He tried to ignore the question hammering through his brain but the truth of his actions was as clear as the scowl he could see in his reflection in the gym's mirrors.

*Are you invested in this?* When he'd blurted those words out last night, he'd been stunned by the need to hear her answer in the affirmative. Because in that moment he'd realised just how truly invested he was in having Brianna in his life and not just as his personal assistant. Even now, with suspicion warring with his new-found intentions to trust more and judge less, the thought of not having her around made a red haze cloud his senses.

*You have three days to get me what I need...*

Was it a professional request? Who would be making such a demand of her professionally?

If it was a personal one…

He emitted the deep growl that had been growing in his chest as jealousy spiked through his gut.

At that moment, Brianna walked into the gym and froze. In the mirror, their eyes meshed. The look on his face was fierce and unwelcoming—he knew that. He wasn't surprised when her eyes widened and she hesitated.

'I can come back later if I'm disturbing you.'

With one last, vicious yank on the row bar, he let it go, watched it clatter against the spinning wheel and stood and advanced towards her.

The sight of her in skin-clinging, midriff-baring

Lycra made adrenaline and arousal spike higher. The thought of making another of his myriad sexual fantasies come true pounded through his blood and groin with a ferocity that made him grit his teeth. He barely managed to catch himself from lunging for her, and veered towards the row of treadmills.

'Disturb me. I was in danger of letting my imagination get the better of me.' He gave a smile he knew fell far short of the mark and busied himself with programming the treadmill next to his. When he was done, he waved her over.

'Thirty minutes okay?' he asked.

He caught the look of wariness on her face as she nodded and approached the machine.

About to set his own programme, he glanced over and was pretty sure he burst a blood vessel when she bent over to stretch.

*'Theos!'* His hiss brought her head up and she slowly straightened.

Her gaze travelled down his chest and dropped to the loose shorts that did nothing to hide the power of her effect of him. When her mouth dropped open, he let out a strained laugh. 'Now you see the power you have over me.'

She stepped onto the treadmill and pressed start. 'You don't sound too happy about it.'

'I like being in control, *agapita*. And you're detonating mine with that tight body of yours.'

He watched the blush creep up from her neck to stain her cheeks. 'It's not exactly a walk in the park for me either, if that helps you?'

Sakis fought to reconcile the blushing, sexually innocent woman in front of him with one who could be capable of duplicity.

*Don't judge before you know the facts...*

Brianna's words flashed through his churning mind. With a deep breath, he started his own machine and began jogging alongside her.

One minute, one full minute, was how long he lasted before he gave in to the urge to glance over at her. The sight of her breasts bouncing beneath her clinging tank top made him groan. Only his ingrained discipline from his professional rowing days stopped him from losing his footing.

But he didn't glance away. He stared his fill. And then he stared some more as his body moved to the spinning treadmill entirely independent of his frenzied thoughts.

She tried to ignore him. But after stumbling a fourth time, she used the handlebars to raise herself and planted her feet on the stationary part of the machine.

'Sakis, please stop doing that. I can't concentrate.'

He blew out a breath and slammed his hand on the stop button. 'Then let's both end this before one of us does themselves an injury.' He reached over and did the same to her machine. 'If you want a workout, I can think of a much better one.'

*'Sakis!'*

'I can't think why I let you call me Mr Pantelides for the last eighteen months, when the sound of my name on your lips makes me harder than I've ever been in my life.'

The gurgling sound she made was somewhere between outrage and reproach as he swung her into his arms, but her arms curved around his neck all the same.

'Should I even ask where you're taking me?'

'I'd love nothing better than to bend you over the handlebars of that treadmill, but I don't have a condom down here, and I can't risk one of my executives walking in on us. My steam room will have to suffice this time.'

He made short work of getting her into his shower to sluice off their sweat before he pushed her into the smoky interior of his private steam room.

He ruthlessly ignored the mocking voice that

suggested he was hiding behind sex instead of confronting her about the text.

But, as he pulled her astride him and plunged deep inside her, Sakis knew he would have to confront her sooner rather than later. He refused to allow suspicion to eat away at him. He'd found a precious peace of mind in her arms this past couple of days and he refused to let distrust and shadows of the past erode it.

Her arms tightened round him as her climax gathered.

'Oh God, Sakis. It feels so good,' she sobbed against his neck.

His own control cracked wider. 'Yes, *agapita*. It would be a shame if something came along and ruined it.' His hand slid into her hair and brought her head up so he could look into her eyes. 'Wouldn't it?' He pushed higher insider her, possessing her completely.

Her lips parted in a pre-climactic gasp as her muscles gripped him tight. 'Yes.'

'Good. Then let's keep that from happening, yes?'

The touch of confusion that clouded her eyes was washed away a second later with the onset of ecstatic wonder that transformed her face from stunning to exquisitely beautiful.

He groaned deep as her convulsions triggered his own release, making him loosen his possessive hold on her. Her head fell back onto his shoulder and it was all he could do to hang on as he was plunged into the longest climax of his life.

He walked them back into the shower as spasms continued to seize her frame.

In silence, he washed her, then himself, all the while aware of the puzzled glances she sent his way.

They made it as far as his bedroom before she rounded on him.

'Is this tense silent treatment part of your morning-after ritual or is there something going on here I should know about?'

He damned his suspicious nature and his inability to shake his gut's warning. His gaze swung past the temptation of her wet, towel-clad body to the bedside table and he tensed further when he saw her phone.

*She'd seen the message.*

'Sakis?'

He met her troubled blue gaze. 'I start negotiations on the China oil deal this morning and they're not the best customers to deal with at the best of times. In light of what's happened, I want nothing to impede this deal.'

Her brow cleared. 'Oh. Well, I don't see anything that will hinder your negotiations.'

His chest lightened at the reassurance then immediately tightened at the thought that the message had been personal, from a man who viewed himself in a position to make demands from the woman Sakis had claimed as his lover. It struck home again just how little he really knew Brianna Moneypenny. Or was it *Anna*?

Sucking in a deep breath, he went to his drawer and pulled out a pair of boxers. 'Are you sure? The last thing we need are skeletons popping out of closets right now. I think my company's had enough of those to last a millennium.'

Her pause lasted a few seconds, but it felt like years to him. 'I'm sure.'

He turned. 'Good.'

When he saw her catch her lower lip between her teeth, his pulse spiked. *Theos*, how could he crave her again after the many times he'd taken her last night and the intense orgasm he'd experienced with her barely fifteen minutes ago? He mentally shook his head, turned away and carried on dressing. If he gave in to his need, they'd never leave this room.

He heard the towel slide from her body and his fingers clenched around his socks.

'So...this is about the Chinese deal and has nothing to do with...with what's happened between us?'

He shoved his leg into his trousers with more force than was necessary. 'I made my feeling clear on that score, *agapita*. You haven't forgotten already, have you?'

'No, I haven't.'

Was that a tremble in her voice? Every instinct screamed at him to ask her about the text.

Private or not, if Brianna was hiding something should he not confront her about it now rather than later?

Heartbeat accelerating wildly, he shrugged on his shirt and faced her.

'Great. Then do you mind telling me what that text on your phone is all about?'

*He knows!*

It took every single ounce of control Brianna could summon not to let out the cry of anguish that ripped through her chest.

'The text?' She hated the breathless prevarication but she needed to buy herself more time.

'Your phone rang in the middle of the night. Someone asked for Anna then hung up. Then the text came. Care to explain?'

*No, no, no,* she wasn't ready. She'd woken up this morning and had lain in the bed knowing without a shadow of a doubt that she'd fallen for Sakis. And also that she needed to come clean and throw herself at his mercy. But she hadn't planned to do it now. Not when Sakis had so much on his plate. She'd planned to type up her resignation then hand it to him with a confession about her past in the hope that he would choose forgiveness over condemnation for her lie about who she really was.

'Brianna?' Sakis's voice was as cold as his expression.

Despair washed over her. 'It's a friend… He wants a favour from me.'

He frowned. 'A *favour.* And he calls you at three in the morning? What sort of favour?'

'Help with his…his work.'

His frown intensified. 'So it wasn't a personal call?'

That she could answer without flinching at the half-truth. 'No.'

Her breath caught as he stalked to where she stood. The sight of him, standing so close with his shirt loose and his ridged chest within touchable distance, made heat spike through her.

'He's not from a competitor, is he? He's not trying to poach you?'

'He's not trying to poach me, no.'

His hand tugged her chin up until her face was exposed to his scrutiny. Whatever he saw there must have satisfied him because after a minute he nodded. Tugging her to him, he grabbed the towel she barely held together and whisked it from her body. He sealed her mouth with his and then proceeded to explore her exposed body with demanding hands. Just when she thought she would expire from need, he set her free.

'That's good to know because otherwise I'd have hunted this man down and torn him limb to limb, as I promised. Now, go and get dressed. And wear one of those no-nonsense suits. It'll kill me to imagine what's underneath it but at least outwardly it'll keep me from jumping you every time you walk into my office.'

A ragged gasp left her at the reprieve she'd been granted and the cowardly way she'd grasped it. In a way, it was a testament to just how pressured Sakis was that he hadn't probed deeper.

*Or it could be that he's beginning to trust you?*

Anguish made her feet slow as she collected her clothes from last night and went into her suite. She'd been granted a reprieve, yes, but had she rendered her eventual confession worthless by not admitting the truth now? Because surely, once she told Sakis just who'd texted her, he'd damn her for ever?

She loved him. Everything about Sakis made her heart beat faster and her soul ache with regret that they hadn't met in another time…a time before she'd been forced to hide her past and unknowingly compromise her future.

Her phone buzzed as she stepped into the grey-and- black platform heels that matched her grey Versace suit.

She knew who it was before she pressed 'answer'.

'I need more time,' she blurted before he'd finished speaking.

Silence. 'You haven't been found out, have you?' Greg demanded.

Brianna sank down onto the hard seat of the dressing stool in her suite's walk-in closet. 'No, but you calling and texting me at three a.m. doesn't help.'

'If you haven't been found out then what's the problem?' he fired back.

'I just… There's a lot of attention on me right now. I need to make sure I do things properly or this will end badly…for both of us.' Her skin burned with each lie. And any minute she suspected the heavens to crack open and lightning to strike her down.

He gave an irritated sigh. 'I have to go out of town unexpectedly. I could be a few days, maybe a week. You have until I get back to get me the information I need. If you don't have it on my return, it's game over.' His tone vibrated with dark menace. 'Word of warning—don't test me, Anna.'

The name scoured across her senses, making her flinch. She was no longer Anna Simpson. Deciding to change her name had been a step in reinventing herself but it wasn't until she'd seen herself through Sakis's eyes that she'd felt truly reborn.

He'd called her amazing yesterday. And throughout the night he'd shown her a powerful ecstasy beyond the physical, made more wonderful because of her feelings for him.

The thought of living without him, of walking away, sent a poker-hot lance of pain through her heart. She was still silently mourning losing Sakis when she walked into the dining room.

The sight of the assorted platters of pancakes, waffles, chocolate and strawberry syrup and endless more condiments made tears prickle her eyes.

Sakis sauntered towards her, one eyebrow raised. 'We made love long and hard last night, and not once did you cry. I'm trying very hard not to let my ego be dented by the fact that it's the sight of pancakes for breakfast that makes you cry and not our lovemaking.'

'I... It's not... No one's ever done anything like this for me,' she finally blurted.

His expression morphed from teasing to compassionate in a heartbeat. 'It's the least of what you deserve, *glikia mou*.' Cupping her face, he sealed his mouth over hers.

*Tell him. Tell him now.*

But how could she tell him about Greg without it all coming out wrong? And how could she confess her love without it sounding like a tool with which to beg his forgiveness?

She'd been gifted extra time with him. And she selfishly, desperately, wanted that time. Maybe she could use it to show him how much he meant to her.

*Action, not words.*

Clutching his nape, she deepened the kiss until he groaned and reluctantly pulled away.

'For kisses like that, you can have pancakes every day. And, before you mention calories, I assure you the workout you'll get in my bed will ensure calories are never an issue.'

He laughed at the flames creeping into her face,

helped her into her seat and forked blueberry pancakes onto her plate.

Sunlight slanted through the windows on a bright London morning, throwing his stunning looks into sharp relief.

His grin as he watched her eat made her heart lift and tighten at the same time. When the look turned smouldering, her belly clenched hard with need.

His buzzing phone ripped through the sensual atmosphere. Sighing, he answered and let the world intrude. Taking the lift down—after a strategic pause, when he kissed her senseless and threatened to take her where she stood if she didn't stop casting him glances from under her lashes—their day swung into full flow.

When at six o'clock he bellowed her name, she entered his office, tablet fired up and ready. His tense expression made her freeze.

'We've tracked him down to Thailand.'

'Captain Lowell?'

He nodded.

'So he's alive?'

'As of yesterday, yes. Although the authorities think there may be someone else besides my security people after him.' His face settled into grimmer lines.

It couldn't be Greg…could it? Nervously, she

licked her lips. 'What do you need me to do?' she asked.

'Nothing for the moment. I'm waiting for the lawyers to apprise me of the full situation, then I'll take it from there.'

'What about the party you wanted me to organise for the crew? Do you want me to cancel it?' She'd been liaising with event organisers all day for the company party Sakis intended to host in Greece.

'No. The party goes ahead. The crew and the volunteers deserve it for the hard work they've put in. I'm not prepared to let one man derail the well-being of my other employees.'

'What about Lowell's wife? Are you going to tell her you've found him?'

A look of distress crossed his face and she knew he was remembering his own mother's situation when the press and gossip-mongers had torn her life apart. 'I don't like keeping her in the dark, but I don't want to cause her pain by revealing half-facts. I'll contact her when we know the full details.'

She nodded and started to return to her desk. 'I'll carry on with arrangements to fly the crew to Greece, then.'

'Wait,' he commanded. He strode to where she stood and kissed her, quick and hard. 'When this is all over, I'm taking you to my Swiss chalet. We'll lock the door behind us and gorge on each other for a week. If one week proves unsatisfactory, we'll take another, and another, until we're too sated to move. Then and only then will we let the world back in. Agreed?'

Her heart skipped several beats. By the time this was over, she'd be gone. But she nodded anyway and hurried back to her desk.

Sinking into her chair, she clenched her shaking hands into fists and fought to stop the unrelenting waves of pain and despair that threatened to drown her.

Eventually, she managed to place a thin veil over her emotions, enough to function for the rest of the day.

The news that Lowell had been arrested and was refusing to cooperate threw the rest of the night into disarray. At one a.m., Sakis stopped pacing long enough to pull her up from the seat on the other side of the sofa where she was busy putting together the itinerary for the next day.

'Go to bed, *agapita*.'

Unable to stop herself, she swayed towards his hard warmth. 'Alone?'

His lips trailed over her cheek to the corner of

her mouth. 'I'll join you as soon as I have the latest update from the lawyers.'

By the time he joined her an hour later, Brianna was almost delirious with need. As he took her on another sheet-burning journey of bliss, she knew without a doubt that, no matter where she went, her heart would always belong to Sakis Pantelides.

## CHAPTER ELEVEN

SAKIS'S PRIVATE GREEK home was a sun-baked slice of bliss that rose from stunning turquoise waters west of the Ionian Islands. Traditionally built and whitewashed in true Greek style, the large villa nevertheless boasted extensive modern designs: the swimming pool had been designed around the villa and traversed under the indoor-to-outdoor living room, reflecting Sakis's love of water.

On her first night here two days ago, Brianna had walked out of her bedroom to find herself faced with an immense mobile hot-tub on her terrace, in which had resided a smug, gloriously naked Sakis with two crystal glasses and vintage champagne chilling on ice next to his elbow. But, if there was one thing she loved about Sakis's island retreat, it was the peace and tranquillity.

Although on this particular Sunday, with teeming bodies enjoying the unfettered generosity of their host, the island paradise was more island rave.

Brianna stood away from the crowd, absently

keeping an eye on a couple of employees who were bent on getting hammered as quickly as possible.

Her phone buzzed in her hand and her heart contracted.

*Need update, pronto. G.*

Greg's texts had got increasingly frequent and terse in the last day. Although she'd managed to fob him off with non-answers, she was fast running out of time. From experience, she knew his patience would only hold out for so long.

She fired back an inadequate *'Soon'*, a cold shiver coursing through her veins despite the fierce summer sun.

She'd greedily grasped the chance to spend some more time with Sakis. But, like sand through an hourglass, it had inevitably run out.

Looking over to where the man who'd taken over one-hundred per cent of her waking thoughts stood with his two brothers, her insides twisted.

The three brothers were gorgeous in their own rights. But, to her, Sakis stood head and shoulders above Ari and Theo.

It had nothing to do with the way his lips curved when he smiled, or the way a lock of hair fell over his forehead when he nodded to something Theo was saying to him…

No, there was a presence about him, an aura of strength and self-containment, that struck a deep place inside her. And the fierce protectiveness he'd displayed towards those loyal to him made her heart ache.

How would it have felt to be loved and cherished by a man such as him? Tears prickled her eyes at the thought that she'd never find out; never know how it would feel to be loved just once by somebody worth giving her own love to.

Her phone buzzed again.

*How soon?????? Answer me now!*

In a fit of anger and torment, she turned it off and dashed blindly towards the steps that led to the beach. Tears blurred her vision but she forged ahead, cursing fate for handing her what she most wanted with one hand and ruthlessly taking it away with the other.

Of course, the beach was occupied with more Pantelides Inc. employees. She plastered on a smile and answered greetings, but continued to walk until the sound of partying and music was far behind her.

Locating a rough, flat rock, she sank down and let the tears she'd held back flow. By the time she was wrung dry, her decision had solidified in her chest.

'So, how's your wonder woman doing?'

Sakis barely managed to stop his teeth from gnashing loudly at Ari's dry query.

'If you don't want me to put a dent in that already messed up face of yours, I suggest you watch your mouth.' He cursed the rough intensity of his tone the moment he spoke.

Sure enough, both Ari's and Theo's eyebrows shot up. A second later, Theo chuckled and nudged their oldest brother. 'The last time he reacted so violently about a girl was when I suggested I bring a lollipop to Iyana when we were kids. I barely managed to avoid being flattened when he tried to run me down with his bike. You better watch out, Ari.'

'Shut the hell up, Theo.' Sakis's mood darkened further as his brothers laughed some more at his expense.

He downed more champagne and raised his head in time to catch Ari's narrow-eyed stare. Staring back defiantly, he watched Ari's mouth drop open.

'Damn it, you've done it, haven't you? You've

slept with her. *Theos*, don't you have any brains in that head of yours?'

Theo let out another rich chuckle. 'Depends on which head you're talking about, bro.'

Sakis released the growl that'd been lurking in his chest for what felt like days. 'I'm warning you both, stay the hell out of my personal life.'

'Or what?' Theo countered. 'I recall you taking delight in causing havoc in mine more than a few times. You sent flowers to that crazy woman you knew I was trying as hard as hell to cut out of my life. And remember that time you stole my phone and used it to sex-text the wrestler brother of that model I was dating? I couldn't return to my apartment for a week because he'd camped outside my building. Payback's a bitch, bro, and I'm only getting started.'

He swallowed the searing response because he knew that what was eating at him wasn't his brothers' ribbing.

It was Brianna. And the secret text messages she was still receiving.

She believed he didn't notice her apprehension every time her phone pinged.

Hell, she'd left his bed at five a.m. this morning. When he'd demanded she come back to bed, she'd waved him away with some excuse about making sure everything was in hand for the party.

*Five a.m.! Yeah, shocking. Wasn't that the same time you interviewed her for her job?*

He smothered the mocking voice and stared into the golden bubbles. This had gone on long enough. He'd swallowed her explanation without probing too deeply. Tonight, after the party, he'd find out what the hell was making her so jumpy. And then he'd fix it. He wanted her undivided attention on him and he sure as hell didn't want her leaving him in bed at the crack of dawn to go do…whatever the hell…

'You're giving us the silent treatment? Really? Wow, you must have it bad!' Theo mocked.

'Sweet mother of— So what if I have a thing for her, hmm?' he demanded wildly.

'Some of us would wonder how many times you had to be burned before you learned your lesson,' Ari said, his gaze and his words holding a steady warning that made Sakis's heart slide to his toes.

'She's not like that, Ari. I…trust her.' It was true. Somehow she'd wormed her way in and embedded herself deep in a place he'd thought dead after his father's betrayal. And, *Theos*, it felt…right. It felt good. He didn't feel so desolate, so bitter any more. And he planned to hang on to it.

'Are you sure?' Ari probed.

Righteous anger rose on Brianna's behalf but he stopped himself from venting it. His brothers were only looking out for him.

He wanted to tell them they didn't need to. But a tiny niggling stopped him. What if they did…?

Brushing the thought away, he turned towards Theo, readying himself for more ribbing.

But his brother's face had turned serious. 'Are the investigators close to wrapping up the Lowell issue?' Theo asked.

The other source of his frustration made his nape tighten. 'Not yet. They think there's a third party at play. Lowell may have been double-dealing both Moorecroft and someone else, someone who's keeping him from talking. They've found a paper trail. They should have a name for me in the next twenty-four hours.'

He heard a drunken shout and looked over to see one of his junior executives falling over a pretty blonde. Realising he hadn't spotted Brianna for a while, he frowned. This was the sort of function where she excelled with her organisational skills.

And yet she was nowhere in sight.

'She went that way, towards the beach,' Ari supplied softly.

Sakis looked at his brother and Ari shrugged, an almost resigned understanding in his eyes.

Were his feelings really so obvious? Who cared? Brianna had breached every single barrier he'd put in place around his heart. He craved her when she wasn't around, and he couldn't have enough of her when she was.

Some might call what he was feeling *love*; he preferred to call it… He searched for a suitable description and came up empty. Whatever it was, he'd decided to risk embracing it, see where it took him.

But before that he needed to get to the bottom of what was bothering her.

The junior executive let out another drunken guffaw. The pretty blonde looked ready to burst into tears. Just then a crash came from the other side of the tent.

'Ari, you go take care of Mr Smooth over there. I'll go check out the other thing?' Theo offered.

Nodding gratefully, Sakis discarded his champagne glass and headed towards his other guests. His heart sank when Ari fell into step beside him.

'Are you sure about what you're doing?' he asked.

'I've never been surer.' His answer held a steady certainty that shifted some hitherto unknown weight from his chest. He wanted Brianna in his life.

*Permanently.*

'Then I wish you well, brother.' Deep emotion and gratitude shifted through him when Ari clasped his shoulder. Before he could swallow the lump in his throat and respond, Ari was moving towards the crowd. Within seconds, the junior executive had been banished to the water fountain to sober up and the blonde was blushing under Ari's dry-witted charm.

Sakis looked towards the beach just as Brianna reappeared at the top of the steps.

The sight of her made his breath catch. It was the first time he'd seen her in such an outfit. Her dress was made of light cotton in a red-and-gold material and stopped just above her knees. The sleeveless, cinched-in waist and flared design moved with her seductive sway as she re-entered the crowd and smiled at a greeting.

He was striding towards her before he could stop himself, not that he wanted to stop.

Her head swung towards him and Sakis's jaw clenched when he saw the momentary wariness that clouded her eyes before she blinked it away. By the time he reached her, she had her game face on.

'It's almost time for your speech,' she said.

'I wish to hell I hadn't agreed to make one.' He wanted to take her face in his hands and kiss away whatever was bothering her, office gossip be damned. But she wouldn't welcome that, so he kept his hands to himself.

*Soon,* he promised himself.

'But you have to. They're expecting it.'

'Right…fine.'

He started to turn away.

'Wait.' She stopped him with a hand on his arm, which she dropped quickly, much to his escalating frustration. 'I…I need to talk to you. Tonight, after the party.'

Real trepidation had darkened her eyes. The unease he'd banked but which had never left him since he'd seen that first text roared to life.

He forced a nod and went to give his speech, then for the next hour he mingled with his employees, the volunteers and salvage crew. But he made sure Brianna was glued to his side. Whatever it was that needed to be aired, he wouldn't let it get in the way of what they had.

He breathed a sigh of relief once the boats arrived to ferry his guests to Argostoli, where the chartered flight waited to take them back to London.

Once the last guest had boarded the boat, he headed towards where Brianna was dismissing the catering staff.

*Finally...*

The need to touch her made his fingers tingle as he came within a few feet of her. She looked up and her desolate expression made his insides clench hard.

'Brianna? What the hell is it?'

She shook her head and looked around. 'Not here. Can we...can we go inside?'

Breaching the gap between them, he caught her hand and kissed the back of it as he steered her towards the villa. 'Sure, but whatever this is let's make it quick. I've been waiting since the crack of dawn to make love to you again. I'm not sure how much longer I can last.'

Her sideways glance was ragged and pain-filled, and he felt his heart stutter then triple its beat as trepidation ramped up higher.

He passed Theo and Ari in the hallway and barely noticed their exchanged glances.

Entering his study, he shut the door and turned to her. 'What's on your mind?'

For several seconds, she didn't speak. She looked lost, miserable, like the bottom had gone out of her world. His heart swelled with the need to take away her pain.

'Brianna, *pethi mou*, whatever the hell it is, I can't fix it until I know what it is.'

That got her attention. She slowly shook her head. 'That's just it. I don't think you can fix this, Sakis.'

His palms grew cold. Clenching his fists tight, he waited.

'A few years ago, I worked for Greg Landers.'

The name popped like a firework in his brain. 'Landers? The guy who was working with Moore-croft?'

'Yes. But back then he owned a gas brokerage firm.'

'And?' he demanded, because his gut told him there was more. Much, much more. 'He's the one who's been texting you. He's *G*.' He didn't try to frame it as a question. He knew.

She licked her lips and, despite the fear and desperation clawing through his belly, he couldn't stop his body's sexual reaction. 'Yes.'

Sakis breathed in deep, but the control kept unravelling. It took every ounce of strength he had to remain standing. 'Is he your lover?'

She gasped. 'No!' A look very much like shame crossed her face. 'But he was,' she whispered.

He'd never understood jealousy up until now. Never got why it compelled strong emotion in others. In that moment, he understood. All Sakis could see in that moment was *red*, fiery red anger, and white-hot pain. 'Why does he call you "Anna"?'

'Because that's my name. My real name is Anna Simpson. I changed it to Brianna Moneypenny after…after…'

'After what?'

'After I served just under two years in jail for embezzlement and fraud.'

Ice, sharp and deadly, clenched hard around his chest. 'You went to *jail*? For *fraud*?'

Tears brimmed in her eyes as she nodded.

Sakis couldn't breathe. His whole body had gone numb. He'd been betrayed *again*. And this time by a woman he loved. And, yes, he could finally admit that the feeling was love because nothing else came close to describing his emotions.

He tried to move towards her and absently noted that his feet were carrying him in the other direction. Numbness spread until his whole body felt frozen to the core.

'You lied to me,' he rasped around the pain gripping his throat.

Slowly, she nodded. Then she cleared her throat. 'Yes.'

'You colluded with a criminal to defraud and then you wormed your way into my company and my bed to do it all over again. You were helping him to topple my company, risking the livelihood of thousands of people.' His voice shook, his insides raw with agony.

'No! Please listen—I didn't. I'd never do that to you.'

'How long have you and Landers been involved in your little scheme?' he snarled, his senses reeling.

Her arms stretched out towards him, palms open wide in false supplication. 'There's no scheme, Sakis. Please believe me.'

His frozen heart twisted painfully. '*Believe you?* That's a joke, right? How long, Brianna?'

Guilt, raw and glaring, slashed across her whitened features. In that moment, Sakis felt as if he'd been turned to stone then smashed into a million pieces.

'I…I've known about it since that last night at Point Noire.'

'And this abrupt confession? You knew it was only a matter of time before the investigators sniffed you both out, didn't you?'

Brianna couldn't stop the distressed cry that

ripped from her throat. 'I wanted to tell you. But I…I didn't want to lose you.'

His devilish laugh sliced through her chest, shredding her already bleeding heart. 'You didn't want to lose me, so you thought you'd do the one thing guaranteed to make that happen? For a woman whose intelligence I once valued, that's shockingly stupid.'

She flinched.

He barely blinked at her pain. 'So, what was the plan? I want to hear it. In detail.'

'Greg wanted information to help him in a new takeover bid: shareholding percentages, personal information about board members to give him an edge.'

His grip on the corner of his desk tightened until his knuckles whitened. 'And you fed him this information? Come clean now because I *will* find out.'

'No! I wouldn't… I'd never…' She stopped and swallowed down the sob that threatened to choke her. 'I know it's too late for me to make you believe me but—'

'What did you expect to receive in return?' he ground out chillingly.

'Nothing! I wanted no part of it. Greg was blackmailing me. He found out I'd changed my name and threatened to expose me.'

'Right; next you'll be telling me you were framed the first time round too.'

'I was!'

'You mean a jury didn't find you guilty and a judge didn't sentence you?' Sakis's numbness was receding and pure rage was taking its place. He welcomed the painful sting in his legs and arms, welcomed the surge of power it brought.

'They did, but Greg had engineered it and made sure I took the fall.'

'How?'

Her tongue darted out to lick her lips. Sakis felt the lash of desire and crushed it dead. 'I signed some papers he asked me to and—'

'Did he force you to?'

'What?'

'You say you signed papers, which I assume implicated you. Did he force you to sign them? Did he stand over you with a gun or threaten you in any way?'

'Um…no, he didn't. He tricked me.'

His disbelieving snort stopped the flow of her words. 'You expect me to believe that the ruthlessly efficient executive assistant who's been in my employ these last eighteen months was the same person who would sign papers without first checking them in triplicate? I assume you were so in love with him, you believed every saintly word that fell from his lips?'

She flinched but remained silent and her hands dropped.

Sakis was glad his rage had ravaged every other emotion otherwise he'd have felt the drowning desolation of that silent confirmation. The woman he loved…loved someone else.

Jerking to his feet, he rounded his desk and called his head of security. Once he'd hung up, he stared down at the papers on his desk, willing his frozen mind to focus. 'Give me your phone.'

She frowned. 'What?'

'Your phone. I know you've got it in your pocket. Hand it over.'

Almost in a daze, she did as he asked. 'What are you going to do with it?'

He threw it in his desk drawer, locked it and pocketed the key. 'As of right now, it's evidence of your duplicity. I'll hand it over to the police when the time is right.'

She sucked in a frightened breath. 'No! Please, Sakis. I can't…I can't go back to prison.'

Despite thinking he was too numb to feel, the

torment and horror in her eyes sent a shaft of pain through him.

His gaze dropped to her hip, to the place where her scar resided. 'That's where you sustained that injury, wasn't it? In jail?' he asked, feeling another shot of scalding pain.

'Yes. I was attacked.'

*Theos!* He turned to face the window so she wouldn't see his eyes clamp shut or the steadying breath he took.

When he heard the knock on his door, relief flooded him. Sheldon entered and Sakis shoved unsteady hands deeper into his pocket and turned around.

'Escort Miss *Moneypenny* off my property. Put her on the same plane returning the other company employees. I want her under twenty-four-hour guard until you hear from me. If she tries to run, you have my permission to physically restrain her and call the police. Is that understood?'

A stunned Sheldon nodded. 'Yes, sir.'

'Sakis, I know you don't believe me, but please be careful. Greg's a slippery bastard.'

He didn't turn around.

'Sakis!' Her desperate plea made him flinch but her betrayal cut too deep.

Nevertheless, he allowed himself one last look.

Her face was devoid of colour and her lips trembled uncontrollably. But her eyes, even though they pleaded with him, held a condemnation that made his fists curl in his pockets.

Sakis wasn't sure how long he stood there. It might have been minutes, it might have been hours.

When his door was thrust open, he turned slowly, his body feeling alien and frozen.

'Is everything okay?' Ari asked as he sauntered in, Theo close behind. There was an almost pitying note in his voice that made Sakis's belly clench hard.

'No, everything is *not* okay.'

'Ah, that's too bad, brother. Because all hell's broken loose.'

## CHAPTER TWELVE

BRIANNA DRAGGED HERSELF out of bed and walked to her window, hoping for a miracle but knowing hope was useless.

Sure enough, Sakis's guard dog was in place in the dark SUV, just like he'd been for the last three days. She didn't bother looking out of her kitchen window because she knew there would be another SUV stationed in the back alley behind her building, should she get the notion of flinging herself out of her second-floor apartment window and making a run for it.

Forcing herself to enter her kitchen and turn on the kettle, she sagged against the counter and tried to breathe through the waves of pain that had become her endless reality since she'd been marched from Sakis's Greek office.

She clamped her eyes shut to block out the look on his face after her confession.

*You lied to me.*

Such simple words, yet with those words her

world had fallen apart. Because there was no going back. Sakis would always see her as the woman who'd worked her way into his bed only to betray him, especially when she'd known just how much betrayal and lies had ruined his childhood.

The kettle whistled. About to grab a mug from the cupboard, she heard the heavy slam of a car door, followed almost immediately by another. When several followed, she set the mug down and moved closer to the window.

The sight of a paparazzo clinging to the side of a cherry picker as it rose to her window was so comical, she almost laughed. When he raised his camera and aimed it towards her, Brianna dived for her kitchen floor. Through the window she'd opened to let in the non-existent summer breeze, she heard him shout her name.

'Do you have a comment on the allegations against you, Miss Simpson?'

Crawling on her belly, she made her way to her hallway just as someone leaned on her doorbell.

The realisation that Sakis had truly thrown her to the wolves sent a lance of pain through her, holding her immobile for a full minute, until her pride kicked in.

She refused to hide away like a criminal. And she refused to be trapped in her own home.

If nothing else, she had a right to defend herself. Gritting her teeth for strength, and ignoring the incessant, maddening trill of her doorbell, she dashed into her room.

Grabbing the first set of clothes that came to hand, she pulled them on. Unfortunately, trainers and her suit didn't go, so she forced her feet into four-inch heels, grabbed her bag and pulled a brush through her hair.

She opened the door and shot past Sakis's shocked guards before they had a chance to stop her.

'Miss Moneypenny, wait!'

She rounded on them as they caught up with her at the top of the stairs. 'Lay a finger on me, and *I'll* be the one calling the police. I'll hit you with assault charges so fast, you'll wonder what century it is.' She felt a bolt of satisfaction when they gingerly stepped back.

She hurried down the stairs, noting that they gave hot pursuit but didn't attempt to restrain her.

The glare of morning sunlight coupled with what seemed like a thousand camera flashes momentarily blinded her.

Questions similar to what the first cherry-picker-riding pap had flung at her came her way, but she'd been doing her job long enough to know never to answer tabloid questions.

With her sight adjusted, she plunged through the crowd and headed for the high street two hundred yards away. When she heard the soft whirr of an engine beside her, she didn't turn around.

'What the hell do you think you're doing, making yourself paparazzi bait?' came the rough demand as rougher hands grasped her arms.

Brianna's heart lurched. The sight of him, right there in front of her, fried her brain cells with pleasure and pain so strong she couldn't breathe for a few precious seconds.

She'd missed him. *God, she'd missed him.*

Then memories of their last meeting smashed through. Sucking in a painful breath, she pulled herself away. 'Nothing that concerns you any longer, Sakis.'

He caught her elbow. 'Brianna, wait.'

'No. Let me go!' She managed to pry her hand away and walk a few steps before he caught up with her again.

'Didn't my security people warn you about the press headed your way?'

'Why should they have? Wasn't that what you planned?'

The hand he reached out to her shook. Or at

least she *thought* she saw it tremble. She was feeling very shaky herself and could've imagined it. 'No, it wasn't. I had nothing to do with this. Brianna, please come with me. We need to talk,' he said urgently.

'Not in this lifetime. You made your feelings about me *abundantly* clear—' She gave a yelp of shock as Sakis pulled her in the limo. 'What the hell—?'

'The paparazzi are increasing by the second. My security won't be able to hold them back for much longer. And I really need to talk to you. *Please*,' he tagged on in a ragged voice.

The mouth she'd opened to blast him with clamped shut again. Glancing closer at him, she noticed the shadows in his eyes and the pinched skin bracketing his lips. Against her better judgement, her heart lurched but she still pulled away until her back was braced against the door. He saw her retreat and his lips firmed.

'You have two minutes, then I'm getting out of this car.'

Before she'd finished speaking, the car was rolling forward. Half a minute later, they were in a school yard three streets away parked in front of a familiar aircraft.

'You landed your helicopter on a school compound in the middle of London?' she asked as he helped her out of the car.

'Technically, this isn't the middle of London, and the school is shut for the holidays. I'll pay whatever fine is levied and, if I have to go jail, well, it'll be worth it.'

'*What* will be worth it?'

He didn't respond, only held the door to the chopper open. With the paparazzi within sniffing distance, it would be only a matter of time before they pounced again.

She got in. Sakis followed her. When he reached over to help her buckle her seatbelt, she shook her head. Having him this close was already shredding her insides. His touch would completely annihilate her.

The journey to Pantelides Towers was conducted in silence. So was the journey in the lift that took them to his penthouse.

'What am I doing here, Sakis?'

He closed his eyes for a second and Brianna remembered how he'd said the sound of his name on her lips made him feel. But that had all been an illusion. Because his unforgiving heart had cast her away from him with the precision of a surgeon wielding a scalpel.

'Where were you going when you left her your apartment?'

'None of your damned business. You can't push me around any more, Sakis. My life is my own—but go ahead, do your worst. I'll fight whatever charges you bring against me. If I lose, so be it. But from here on in, *I* control my destiny.'

She ground to a halt, her breath rushing in and out. Sakis glanced from her face to the phone he'd taken from his pocket.

Belatedly, she realised it was her phone. 'What are you still doing with that? I thought you were going to turn it over to the authorities.' Her voice trembled but she raised her chin and glared at him.

'Not after I saw what was on it.'

'What…what did you see?'

He walked slowly towards her, contrition and desperation in his eyes as he held the screen in front of her face.

'I saw this.' The shaken reverence in his voice sent an electrified current through her. Almost fearing to, she glanced down.

*You can go rot in hell, Greg. You once tricked me into taking the fall for something you did. And now you want me to betray the man I love? No chance.*

She looked up from the screen, her heart hammering against her ribs. 'So what? You shouldn't believe everything you read. For all you know, I could've sent that text just to throw you off the scent.'

He glanced down at the screen again and stared at the words as if imprinting them on his brain for all time. 'Then why did you warn me about him?'

She shrugged.

'Brianna, Greg confessed that he coerced you into signing the papers he used to divert funds into his offshore account.'

Shock ricocheted through her body. 'He came clean? Why?'

'He's facing charges in three countries for bribing Lowell to crash the tanker. I told him I would delay the Greek charges if he gave me any useful information. He gave up the dates, figures and codes to his Cayman Islands accounts and confessed he tricked you into helping him siphon off the money.'

The handbag she clutched slipped from her fingers. 'So...you believe me?'

Pain washed over his face. 'Wasting time feeling sorry for myself gave Landers time to spill your real identity to the tabloids. But I shouldn't have doubted you in the first place.'

'I don't really care that everyone knows who I was. And, given the overwhelming evidence, you would've been a saint not to doubt me.'

He flung the phone away and stalked to where she stood. He started to reach for her then clasped both hands behind his nape. 'Then I should damn well have applied for sainthood. What he did to you...what *I* did...*Theos*, I'm even surprised you agreed to come here with me.'

'I was heading here anyway,' she confessed.

Surprise flared in his eyes, along with hope. 'You were?'

'Don't flatter yourself, Sakis. I wasn't on my way to beg you for my life back, if that's what you think. I was coming to clear my desk, or ask security to clear it for me if I was still barred from entering these hallowed grounds.'

'You're not barred. You'll *never* be barred, Brianna.'

'You don't have to call me that. You know who I am now.'

The hard shake of his head made a lock of hair fall over his eyes. 'You'll always be Brianna to me. She was the woman I fell in love with. The woman who possesses more strength and integrity in her little finger than anyone else I know. The woman

I stupidly discarded before I got the chance to tell her how much I love her and treasure her.'

Her legs finally gave way beneath her. Sakis caught her before she crumpled onto the sofa. They fell back together. His gaze dropped to her mouth that had fallen open with wordless wonder, and he groaned. 'I know what I did was unforgivable but I want to try all the same to make it up—'

'You love me.'

'To you. Name your price. Anything you want, I'll give it. I've already put steps in place to have your conviction revoked—'

*'You love me?'*

He paused and gave a solemn nod but it was the adoration in his eyes that struck pure, healing happiness into her heart. 'I love you more than I desire my next breath. I need you in my life. I'll do anything, *anything,* to have you back, *agapita*.'

'What does that mean?'

'What does what...? Oh—*agapita*? It means "beloved".'

She pulled back. 'But you started calling me that even before we slept together. It was that day when you took me for pancakes.'

He seemed startled by the remark. Then a smile warmed his stricken face. 'I think my subconscious was telling me how I felt about you.'

She caressed a hand down his rough jaw. 'When did the rest of you catch up?'

'In Greece, after I withstood Ari and Theo's ribbing and I admitted that I didn't want to live without you. I intended to tell you after the party.'

'Tell me again now.'

He repeated it, then pulled back after kissing her senseless, his gaze dark with a vulnerability she'd never seen. 'Can you ever forgive me for what I did?'

His cheeks were warm and vibrant beneath her hands. 'You took steps to find out the truth about what happened to me. You could've walked away and condemned me, but you came back for me. I told you about my past, about my mother, and you didn't judge me or make me feel worthless. I loved you for that. More than I already did before I sent Greg that text.'

The shock on his face made her smile. It was the shock that made her get away with kissing him thoroughly before the alpha male in him took over. When he pulled away from her, she gave a groan of protest.

'Do you have one of those go bags ready for a trip? If you don't, we'll manage, but we need to leave now.'

'I do, but—?'

He was up and striding towards her suite before she could finish the question. He returned, two bags in one hand and the other stretched out to her.

'Where are we going?' Hurriedly, she straightened her clothes and hair.

'I've blocked off my calendar for a month. I believe there's a Swiss chalet waiting for us.'

'You think a month is going to be enough?' Happiness made her saucy, she discovered.

Pulling her close, he kissed her until they were both breathless. 'No chance. But it's a damned good start.'

The fire roared away in the enormous stone hearth as Sakis pulled the luxury throw closer around them and fed her oysters from the shell. Brianna wrinkled her nose at the peculiar taste.

'Don't worry, *agapita*. You get used to it after a while.'

'I don't think I'll ever get used to it; I'm not afraid to admit this is one lost cause to me.'

His eyes darkened. 'I'm glad you didn't condemn me as a lost cause.'

'How could I, when you tell me you fought your own board for me? How hellish was it to keep them from crucifying me?'

'I almost resigned at one point but, when I

pointed out that *you* deserved all the credit because you saved the company from another stock market slide, they came round to my way of thinking.'

Her eyes widened. 'I did?'

He nodded. 'Telling me about Greg saved the investigators a lot of time. Once we knew who we were looking for, finding him hiding away in Thailand with Lowell was easy. Didn't you see the arrests on the news?'

'Sakis, I could barely get out of bed to feed myself. Watching the news and risking seeing you was too much.'

He froze and jagged pain slashed his features. '*Theos*, I'm so sorry.'

She kissed him then watched him pile more food on her plate. 'You have enough there to feed two armies. I can't possibly eat all of that.'

'Try. I don't like hearing that you didn't eat because of me. I watched my mother wither away from not eating after what my father did to her.'

Pain for him scoured her heart. 'Oh, Sakis…'

He shook his head. 'Eat, *agapita*, and tell me you forgive me.'

'I'll forgive you anything if you keep calling me that.'

After she ate more than was good for her, he stretched her out on the rug and pulled the sheepskin throw off her. Kissing his way down her body, he repeated the endearment over and over again, until she sobbed with need for him.

In the aftermath of their love-making, he brushed the tears from her eyes and kissed her lids.

'I've made you cry with happiness and there're no pancakes in sight. That, *agapita*, is what I call a result.'

* * * * *

**A D'ANGELO LIKE NO OTHER**
Carole Mortimer

**SEDUCED BY THE SULTAN**
Sharon Kendrick

**WHEN CHRISTAKOS MEETS HIS MATCH**
Abby Green

**THE PUREST OF DIAMONDS?**
Susan Stephens

**SECRETS OF A BOLLYWOOD MARRIAGE**
Susanna Carr

**WHAT THE GREEK'S MONEY CAN'T BUY**
Maya Blake

**THE LAST PRINCE OF DAHAAR**
Tara Pammi

**THE SECRET INGREDIENT**
Nina Harrington

**STOLEN KISS FROM A PRINCE**
Teresa Carpenter

**BEHIND THE FILM STAR'S SMILE**
Kate Hardy

**THE RETURN OF MRS JONES**
Jessica Gilmore

*Mills & Boon® Large Print*

*September 2014*

**THE ONLY WOMAN TO DEFY HIM**
Carol Marinelli

**SECRETS OF A RUTHLESS TYCOON**
Cathy Williams

**GAMBLING WITH THE CROWN**
Lynn Raye Harris

**THE FORBIDDEN TOUCH OF SANGUARDO**
Julia James

**ONE NIGHT TO RISK IT ALL**
Maisey Yates

**A CLASH WITH CANNAVARO**
Elizabeth Power

**THE TRUTH ABOUT DE CAMPO**
Jennifer Hayward

**EXPECTING THE PRINCE'S BABY**
Rebecca Winters

**THE MILLIONAIRE'S HOMECOMING**
Cara Colter

**THE HEIR OF THE CASTLE**
Scarlet Wilson

**TWELVE HOURS OF TEMPTATION**
Shoma Narayanan